THE NIGHT WAS COLD BUT SHE WAS WARM . . .

as she dropped her wrapper and slipped in beside Justice. She was a very beautiful, very dangerous woman, and a hell of a sensuous woman too. In a flash of lightning, Ruff saw her smooth bare shoulders, her eager face, and the lovely full breasts which his hands found and stroked. Then she was clinging to him, her mouth searching his, her hands reaching hungrily for him, pausing only long enough to let him wriggle out of his buckskins like a snake shedding its skin.

Yes, Ruff thought as he pulled her to him, she was as deadly dangerous as they came, but right now it was a real pleasure to play her game. . . .

SIGNET Brand Westerns You'll Enjoy

- [ ] **THE DEAD GUN by Ray Hogan.** (#E9026—$1.75)
- [ ] **THE DOOMSDAY TRAIL by Ray Hogan.** (#E9354—$1.75)
- [ ] **THE HELL RAISER by Ray Hogan.** (#E9489—$1.75)*
- [ ] **THE RAPTORS by Ray Hogan.** (#E9124—$1.75)
- [ ] **PILGRIM by Ray Hogan.** (#E9576—$1.75)*
- [ ] **RETURN OF A FIGHTER by Ernest Haycox.** (#E9419—$1.75)
- [ ] **A RIDER OF THE HIGH MESA by Ernest Haycox.**
      (#W8962—$1.50)
- [ ] **SIGNET DOUBLE WESTERN—BRANDON'S POSSE by Ray Hogan and THE HELL MERCHANT by Ray Hogan.**
      (#J8857—$1.95)*
- [ ] **SIGNET DOUBLE WESTERN—THE DEVIL'S GUNHAND by Ray Hogan and THE GUNS OF STINGAREE by Ray Hogan.**
      (#J9355—$1.95)
- [ ] **SIGNET DOUBLE WESTERN—LAWMAN FOR SLAUGHTER VALLEY by Ray Hogan and PASSAGE TO DODGE CITY by Ray Hogan.** (#J9173—$1.95)*
- [ ] **SIGNET DOUBLE WESTERN—THREE CROSS by Ray Hogan and DEPUTY OF VIOLENCE by Ray Hogan.** (#J9501—$1.95)
- [ ] **SIGNET DOUBLE WESTERN—RIM OF THE DESERT by Ernest Haycox and DEAD MAN'S RANGE by Ernest Haycox.**
      (#J9210—$1.95)

* Price slightly higher in Canada

Buy them at your local bookstore or use this convenient coupon for ordering.

THE NEW AMERICAN LIBRARY, INC.,
P.O. Box 999, Bergenfield, New Jersey 07621

Please send me the SIGNET BOOKS I have checked above. I am enclosing
$_____ (please add 50¢ to this order to cover postage and handling).
Send check or money order—no cash or C.O.D.'s. Prices and numbers are
subject to change without notice.

Name _____

Address _____

City_____ State_____ Zip Code_____
Allow 4-6 weeks for delivery.
This offer is subject to withdrawal without notice.

RUFF JUSTICE #1

Sudden Thunder

by

Warren T. Longtree

A SIGNET BOOK

NEW AMERICAN LIBRARY

TIMES MIRROR

PUBLISHER'S NOTE

This novel is a work of fiction. Names, characters, places, and incidents are either the product of the author's imagination or are used fictitiously, and any resemblance to actual persons, living or dead, events, or locales is entirely coincidental.

Copyright © 1981 by The New American Library, Inc.

SIGNET TRADEMARK REG. U.S. PAT. OFF. AND FOREIGN COUNTRIES REGISTERED TRADEMARK—MARCA REGISTRADA HECHO EN CHICAGO, U.S.A.

SIGNET, SIGNET CLASSICS, MENTOR, PLUME, MERIDIAN AND NAL BOOKS are published by The New American Library, Inc., 1633 Broadway, New York, New York 10019

First Printing, September, 1981

1 2 3 4 5 6 7 8 9

PRINTED IN THE UNITED STATES OF AMERICA

1

THE MOON HUNG silver above the rolling hills to the north. The grass was glazed with silver frost. The tall man closed the wooden door to the sod house and drew in the latchstring. He crossed to the bed and slipped in beside Madeline.

There was only the reddish glow of the low-burning fire and the soft breathing of the woman. Justice let his head rest on her breast, hearing the swelling of her heart, his nostrils filled with the earthy woman scent of Madeline.

His finger traced patterns on her breasts, around her taut pink nipples, and he touched his lips to them, taking the nipples into his mouth, first one and then the other, as Madeline lay back, her hands on his head, her eyes shut.

Justice's hands ran along her thighs and found the rising contour of her hip. His lips followed his hands and he kissed her navel, feeling the soft flesh of her abdomen beneath his lips as the woman scent grew stronger.

Shifting slightly, he kissed her hip, the soft inner flesh of her thigh, and he felt her pulse begin to race. Sitting up, he smiled at Madeline. Her hair in yellow profusion across the pillow, her overripe mouth.

1

She was no longer young, but her body was firm, with the lushness which sometimes comes only with maturity.

As he watched she shifted in bed; her eyes flickered open to study his dark silhouette, and she smiled in the darkness.

Justice's hand went again to her thigh, wondering at the softness of it beneath his callused hand. Responding to his touch, Madeline's legs parted slightly, and then a little more as his searching fingers moved through the soft bush between her thighs.

He found the rigid, sensitive tab of flesh there, and he stroked it slowly before allowing his fingers to dip inside of Madeline, finding her warm, dewy.

"Justice," Madeline sighed, and her hands stretched out to him in the darkness. He lay beside her, still touching her inner flesh, and for a moment Madeline's fingers met his, guiding him, touching her own juices on his fingers.

Then she reached out and found his erection, which was warm, throbbing against her thigh. Slowly she took his cock into her hand, her practiced fingers searching him from the base of his shaft to the sensitive head of it, where her fingers patterned tiny, inflaming whorls across his flesh.

She did not want to wait, not on this night, and she rolled to him, her open mouth meeting his, her leg raised. She still held to his erection, and now she positioned it, the head of it just within her warmth, and it inflamed Justice, who kissed her eyes, her throat, her breasts as he slid into Madeline.

Madeline sighed deeply, and she petted his head, feeling him slowly enter her, fill her with a warm glow, and she started swaying against him. Justice's hands went to her hips, between her legs where he felt himself entering her, where he met Madeline's own searching fingers as they explored each other.

Now Madeline's head lolled back and she slowly rolled flat on her back, her knees raised, spreading herself. Justice touched bottom now, and Madeline trembled as he did so. Their pelvises were pressed together, Madeline's warm breath in his ear.

She began to thrust against him, a demanding, hungry thrusting which Justice answered with his own strokes. Her head rolled from side to side now, her mouth half open, her eyes distant as she felt herself rising to a new peak, felt a hot rush of sensation begin to trickle from within and then flow across her pelvis, her hips, rising to her breasts, and she reached up and bit Justice on the shoulder, wanting more, needing more, and he gave it to her.

He stroked her hair, kissed her breasts, throat, lips lightly as he continued to work against her, to sway with her demanding body until Madeline again felt her orgasm building, and in a frantic burst of desire, she kissed him savagely, using her teeth, as her hands clutched his hard-muscled buttocks, and then she came undone, and Justice felt her quiver, tense, utterly relax. His own need had built to an insistent demand, and Madeline felt him tense, felt him rock against her, moving in a slow circle, until suddenly he stopped, rigid, and he penetrated to her depths, filling her with his own climax.

They lay side by side for a long while, touching each other, exchanging tender kisses. She was warm in the cold night, comforting, and now she slept. Justice watched her for a time and then rolled onto his back, his hands behind his head.

He heard the distant howl of a coyote, a crashing of glass from near the barracks, and then it was still again.

He lay watching the last glow of the embers in the hearth for a long, silent hour before finally falling off to a troubled sleep.

The old dream came again, as it always did.

Along the grassy knoll, blood-red flowers grew in a perfect row, and Justice shot them one by one until the last blossom exploded in a fiery wash.

Then, naked, he rode a headless horse across the yellow-grass plains, and behind him rode the hunters—screaming, hurling fiery lances. Then the horse was gone from beneath him and he ran on, stumbling into a deep, terrifying canyon.

Far above he saw their indistinct figures against the skyline. And he heard them growling, laughing as they spilled fire down upon him. He cringed and walked backward into the dark river, but the river too caught fire, and he tried to swim against the terrible current, stretching out a hand to the ghostly woman on the bank.

Her arm was bony, white, and as he clutched at it, her arm came off in his hand and the river swept him away. Laughter thundered down the dark canyon, pursuing him as his skin crackled in the angry flames.

The dream parted and Justice rolled to the side of the bed, head in his hands. His dark hair fell across his face, and he shivered slightly with the predawn cold.

A sliver of gray light leaked through the wall of the low-roofed soddy. Madeline turned a little onto her side and breathed a muffled word.

Justice studied her shadowed body, the breast which had escaped the confines of the bedsheet, the soft curve of her broad hips, the night-tangled blond hair. She slept; she rested.

They were indeed the lucky ones—those to whom sleep brought relief and not the torment of dreams.

Standing, Justice walked to the bureau, rubbing the coldness from his white arms which ended in leathery, sun-browned hands.

Breaking the film of ice from the washbasin, he splashed cold water onto his face, peering through his fingers at the man in the smoky glass of the mirror. Tall, narrow-faced, with flowing dark hair. His nose was perfectly straight, although it had been broken twice. His eyes were red-rimmed, deep blue. An eighteen-inch scar ran across his flat, white ribcage, and two small, nearly round scars showed as dark, dollar-sized blemishes near the collar-bone on the left side.

Justice hung his head over the washbasin, studying the distorted reflection in the water. Then he glanced again, quickly, at the mirror and smiled faintly.

Madeline still slept, and the shaft of gray light creeping under the plank door to the sod house became brighter, wider. Justice searched in his leather pouch for soap and his shaving brush. Then he shaved, standing still naked before the mirror.

Carefully sweeping aside his mustache, which drooped past the jawline, he scraped the dark stubble from his tanned cheeks.

There was a tap at the door, and Justice looked around with surprise. He tried to ignore the knocking, but it continued insistently, and with disgust he walked to the plank door, swinging it wide on its leather hinges.

"Sir . . ." Light flooded the one-room soddy. The young ruddy-faced corporal stood there gawking, looking from the tall, naked man to the bed, where Madeline, suddenly awakened, was sitting with the sheet over her breasts, her hair across her eyes.

"*Sir?* Is *that* the message, corporal?" Justice asked

wryly, and the corporal took an involuntary step backward.

"No, sir."

Justice smiled at the amended message. His eyes lifted to the high log walls of the fort stockade, to the green, mist-shrouded hills beyond the river. Dove going to feed cut dark silhouettes against the early-morning sky.

"*Is* there a message?" Justice prompted. The soldier, who had never encountered a naked legend before, managed it finally.

"Colonel MacEnroe requests your presence as soon as possible, sir."

"Sioux?"

"No, sir, I don't think so," the corporal stammered.

"I'll be along shortly."

Justice closed the door with a sigh. Madeline's eyes were on him now as he crossed the room. "Are you going?" she asked.

"You heard the soldier."

"But you are *going?*"

Madeline rose sleepily from the bed, and she walked to Justice, interrupting his shaving. She leaned nearer to him, and her soft scent filled his nostrils, her hair hung across his chest.

Justice put an arm around her. His hand still held his ebony-handled razor. He touched her lips gently, searching for a spark which he could not find. Brushing back her hair, he kissed her forehead, feeling the pulsing of her blood, the swelling of her breasts against his chest. He smiled and turned back toward the mirror.

"Didn't it mean anything to you?" she asked.

"Yes." There was surprise in his face. "It meant much. You mean much to me, Madeline. I gave you what you wanted; what more do you expect?"

Sullenly she sat down once more on the bed, watching as the tall man finished shaving, as he combed out that fine, long dark hair which any woman would envy.

Without speaking, Justice went to the peg on the wall where his buckskins hung. He slipped into his pants and shirt, which were of white elkskin, decorated with lavish beadwork by Four Dove those many winters ago when he had shared her hogan.

His boots, also of elkskin, also fringed, sat near the rough chair in the corner of the room, and Justice slipped them on, positioning the thin, ivory-handled skinning knife which was sheathed inside the right boot.

Justice wore a beaded gunbelt with the butt of his Colt positioned forward, the other side weighted down by a murderously sharp, stag-handled bowie knife. By the door rested his Spencer rifle, sheathed in a fringed buckskin scabbard.

Madeline watched as he dressed, becoming by layers and degrees the savage, wild thing Ruffin Justice was. Her eyes were bright, but moist. Justice picked up his broad-brimmed white hat and planted it carefully on his head, sweeping back his dark curls.

"God, Justice," she said reverently, "you're a man to look upon."

Justice turned toward her, picking up his saddlebags, his rifle. He smiled briefly, thinly.

"And you are a woman to have been with, Madeline, one to be remembered."

Again Justice kissed her, stroking her hair. He lightly kissed her bare shoulder, and then, touching the brim of his hat, he walked from the room, leaving the door open.

Dooley Dog was beside the threshold, and he

looked up at his master, rising with a yawn to trot after the long-striding plainsman.

Madeline stood in the doorway, the cold wind
washing over her, watching after Justice for a moment longer. The tall man strode away with his back
straight, his boots leaving spade-shaped imprints in the
frosted grass. That funny gray-spotted white dog
tagged along behind, tongue dangling.

The walls of the fort, chiseled against the sky,
seemed distant as she watched; the yellow-gold hills
beyond were barren, cold. With a sigh, Madeline
wrapped the sheet more tightly around her shoulders
and turned back into the rough sod house.

"Frankly, captain," Colonel MacEnroe was saying,
"I would advise you to utterly discourage this expedi-
tion. It is an invitation to slaughter. And we are not
speaking now of military casualties, but of civilians.
If you can imagine the repercussions in Washington . . ."

"May I remind the colonel that it is the Secretary
himself who has authorized this mission?"

"And the military which must bear the responsibil-
ity!" Colonel MacEnroe stood behind the desk, his
face flushed. A square-shouldered man with a narrow
white mustache, he had had a bellyfull of civilian in-
terference during his distinguished career. Well-mean-
ing bureaucrats clogging the mechanism of the
military. At times it was enough to cause the colonel
to sit down and count the days to his retirement.

"I believe this is why you are paid each month," the
man in the corner chair said slowly. "To protect the
public in Dakota Territory."

MacEnroe swallowed a sharp retort. The man he
faced wore a pin-striped suit. A hat perched on his

crossed knee. He smiled insufferably at the colonel. Slowly MacEnroe replied.

"I remind you, Mr. Denton, that the military just now is hard pressed to defend itself in Dakota Territory. I have half of my forces in the field at the moment, chasing—or being chased by—a large band of Oglala Sioux. If you are not aware of the reputation of these red warriors, I would advise you to reread last year's newspapers—"

Denton interrupted impatiently. "I am aware of Colonel Custer's misadventure."

"Misadventure!" MacEnroe was fuming. "I take it, sir, that you were far removed from Dakota during that *misadventure*. That you have never seen the aftermath of such a misadventure, that you have never—"

"Sir," the captain interrupted softly.

Colonel MacEnroe sagged into his chair, his eyes still flashing. Again he looked at the document before him, a request for military escort through to Camas Meadows, five hundred miles distant through thousands of hostile Sioux. He shook his head, wondering what those men in Washington used for brains.

Denton sat placidly in the corner, a man who had probably never been so far as his front gate in Baltimore without an escort. If that were not enough, Denton and his brother had brought along their sisters.

Marguerite Denton sat silently near the door, a dark-eyed beautiful woman of twenty, no more. She smiled brilliantly as MacEnroe glanced her way. The second brother, Amos, stood behind her chair, his face passive, dull.

"I cannot, in good conscience, provide you with a full escort," the colonel said decisively. "It would be a dereliction of duty at this time, under these circumstances."

"But the Secretary—"

"The Secretary has requested an escort," the colonel responded, waving a hand. MacEnroe stood and went to the window, watching A Company drill in the yard for a time. "I will provide you with the best man I have—although I sorely hate to lose him just now."

"One man!" Hugh Denton was apoplectic. "Sir, may I remind you that we have women with us!"

"May I remind you how they got here," Colonel MacEnroe answered bitterly.

"This is an outrage," Denton said, biting off his words. "The Secretary will be informed."

"Please do inform him. Personally and at once, if possible. If you wish, sir, I give you the option of waiting for a more propitious moment, or for more specific orders to arrive from the War Secretary's office. Of course," MacEnroe added, settling once again into his seat, "by the time such orders could arrive in Dakota, you might find yourself gray-headed and myself long retired."

"I can't understand your attitude," Denton went on. "My sisters and my brother and I simply wish to find and return to Baltimore the body of our beloved father, who like yourself, sir, was a career officer, a gallant warrior."

"My attitude," MacEnroe said stonily, "is based on one single fact which you continue to ignore, Mr. Denton. If I allow you to go through to Camas Meadows, which it appears I must . . ." He glanced again at the orders on his desk top. "There will be not *one* deceased Denton to return to Baltimore, but an entire family."

"Nevertheless, I . . ."

The door opened quietly, and Hugh Denton turned toward it. The tall man in fringed buckskins stood there silently. Denton blinked, examining this long-haired apparition.

Marguerite Denton also looked at Justice, but she did not blink. Her eyes stared with frank interest until Justice's cool blue eyes met her own, and then she turned her head away.

"Come in, Ruff," the colonel said.

Justice closed the door and crossed the room, and Marguerite noticed that his boots made barely a sound as he did so. Dark hair curled down the back of his white elkskin shirt, the front of which was brilliantly beaded. The fringes on his shirt and leggings were very long. He cradled his sheathed rifle in his long arms like a beloved infant.

Hugh Denton scratched his ear and shook his head, glancing at his brother, who shrugged in return.

"This is Ruffin T. Justice," the colonel said, standing for the introduction. Justice only nodded, and Hugh seemed relieved.

"Ruff, this is Mr. Hugh Denton, his brother Amos, and Miss Marguerite Denton. They want to find their father's body and return it to their home in Baltimore. Major Denton was killed at Camas Meadows. See them through, will you?"

MacEnroe could barely meet Justice's eyes. He knew what he was asking—the territory was unsettled, alive with hostiles. Justice's face altered as with faint amusement, and he nodded.

"I'll draw supplies," he said. His eyes were on Marguerite in a way which both pleased her and frightened her.

Dooley Dog had plopped down at her feet, and idly she stretched out a hand to pet the little white animal.

"I wouldn't do that," Justice cautioned her. "Dooley Dog does not bark, but he bites."

Marguerite withdrew her hand quickly, trying to decide if he was joking or not. The dog wore a black leather collar, and on it was a silver plate and two smaller ornaments which Marguerite could not make out.

"If that's all, colonel?" Justice said.

"That's all, Ruff. Good luck."

Justice nodded to the Dentons and then strode silently to the door, Dooley Dog jumping up to trail after him.

"One man," Hugh Denton said disgustedly. "And *that* man! Why, he appears nothing if not the fop!"

Colonel MacEnroe's eyes went hard. He stepped around the desk to face Hugh Denton.

"Sir," the officer told Denton, "I said I would give you my best man, and you have him.

"Ruffin Justice knows this country better than any other white man alive. He was with the first party to reenter the Black Hills after Little Bighorn. He has fought beside me, valiantly, in six Indian battles. His Civil War record is remarkable for gallantry.

"But I warn you . . ." MacEnroe lifted a menacing finger. "Justice has fought three duels that I know of, two with bowie knives, his wrist strapped to his opponent's. None of those men is here today. Justice is. Whatever you think of his dress, his . . . unique character, I would advise you most strongly to keep your thoughts to yourself, sir.

"Goodbye." MacEnroe added shortly, stiffly. "Good luck."

Denton blinked, unable to comprehend for a moment that the interview had come to an abrupt end. He bowed slightly to the colonel and then offered his hand to Marguerite, who took it, rising. They walked from the office with Amos trailing, and out into the clear light of morning, a cold wind meeting them.

Across the parade ground a company of men drilled. The hammering of the blacksmith rang out from the shed beside the main gate.

Hugh snipped the end from a cigar and lit it. He stood smoking for a moment, rocking on his heels. The tall man in white elkskin clothes was near the stable, throwing a silver-bright saddle onto the back of a long-legged Appaloosa.

"Well," she asked, "is he the man for it?"

Hugh Denton shrugged, glancing at his sister, whose eyes were riveted on the tall man. "He'd better be," Denton grumbled finally, "or we're all in way over our heads, aren't we?"

Justice tightened the cinches on his saddle, kneeing the startled Appy in the stomach, forcing it to expell the extra air it held.

"Don't be contrary with me, Commodore. I'm expecting enough balkiness from the human people." Affectionately he slapped the Appy's neck and led it from the stableyard.

Dooley Dog had been up on his hind legs, taking a drink from the trough. Now, water flying from his muzzle, he charged after Justice, his stubby legs churning.

From the sutler Justice picked up several hams, coffee, tinned peaches, a hundred rounds of .44s for his Colt and an equal number of .52s for his Spencer repeater.

"Be needing paper and ink, Ruff?" the sutler asked.

"No. I have enough, Wes."

"This all going on your private tab?" the sutler wanted to know. Justice shook his head.

"Colonel's draw."

"Okay. I just wondered." Wes scratched his head

with his stub of a pencil. "Anybody ridin' out just now . . . I sort of like to keep those private tabs cleared up."

"What do I owe you?" Justice asked. From inside his shirt he pulled out a beaded purse.

"Hell, it's only six, seven dollars, Ruff. I just meant . . ."

"You're right." Justice counted out seven dollars. "You never do know when a man's taking his last ride." Then Justice picked up his stores, and with a nod he walked from the sutler's, tossing Dooley Dog a salt biscuit from the barrel.

The Denton wagon was parked around in the shade of the headquarters building, but the Dentons were nowhere to be seen. Justice let down the tailgate and sat his supplies on it. Then he threw back the canvas flap.

There she sat.

A gaunt, black-eyed woman in a white chemise, her hands folded before her, sat rocking in a chair in the back of the Denton wagon. She looked at Justice with eyes as dark and inert as obsidian. Lifeless eyes they were. Her dark hair wound across her shoulders and breasts.

Pretty, she was, or would have been—but for the missing, vital spark. Justice stood staring, transfixed by this frail ghost girl.

"What hand has drawn the veil across thy sight/ And driven from thy soul all conscious light? Poor woman," he breathed.

There was a rough hand on Justice's wrist, and he drew back to face an angered Hugh Denton.

"And is it a part of the scout's job to pry into wagons?"

Justice glanced at the hand which still rested on his wrist and then looked up into Hugh Denton's brown eyes. Slowly Denton released his grip, as if he had been holding a rattler's head.

"I only figured to pack my stores in your wagon," Justice told him. Although his voice was level, there was something in the timbre of it and in the glittering of those blue eyes which made Denton know he had come near to the line.

"Candida is not well, obviously," Denton said.

"This is no place for her," Justice replied.

"Maybe not—but we had no place to leave her. My sister has been like this since the news of Father's death reached us."

Marguerite had come around the wagon, a quilt in her hands, and she glanced from one man to the other curiously. "I was explaining about Candida," Denton said and shrugged. Then he turned and walked away, his teeth working row against row.

"It's been hard on Hugh, on all of us," Marguerite said, and she leaned near to Justice as she said that. He picked up the faint scent of lavender, and he studied the woman before him, the clear eyes and small pink ears, the ringlet of auburn hair which fell across her pale neck.

"Is she all right?" Justice asked, nodding at the wagon.

"She's fine." Marguerite smiled. She placed the folded quilt inside the wagon and tied the flap down once again. "She's ridden from St. Joe like that—the rocker is strapped to the floor. The chair . . . rocking in it seemed her only comfort after Father was killed. Candida would sit by the hour, watching the fire." She shrugged and flashed a smile. "Well, you don't want to hear about all of that."

"Not now. Maybe one of these nights you'll have the time to tell me all about it, about yourself."

"Perhaps." Her lips formed into a thoughtful smile

as she studied the tall man once more. "One of these nights."

Then Justice turned and gathered up the reins to his Appaloosa horse, and he stepped into the saddle. With a nod he turned the horse and rode easily toward the main gate, the little white dog trotting at the Appy's heels.

Marguerite watched him for a time longer, the smile gradually fading from her lips. Hugh was at her shoulder now, and he too watched Justice as he talked to the watchtower guards.

"Well?"

"You may be right, Hugh," Marguerite said. "It just may be that we've bitten off more than we can chew with Mr. Justice."

"We need him," Hugh reminded her. "We need him badly—for now. Keep him happy, Marguerite. Keep his thoughts on other things, will you?"

"That won't be hard from what I hear," Amos Denton said. He stood there grinning, his unshaven cheek stuffed with tobacco. Hugh and Marguerite were interested.

"What did you hear?"

"See that man over there?" Amos lifted his chin to indicate a hugely built, black-bearded man standing in front of the sutler's door, glaring at Justice. "His name's Solomon Turk. Hunts meat for the soldiers. He come back early this mornin' from a hunting trip, saw Justice comin' from his woman's house."

"He looks ready to kill," Marguerite said with a shiver.

"He's ready," Amos agreed. "If you'd of heard him talkin' . . ."

Hugh glanced at Marguerite. Solomon Turk—it was a name to remember. From the front gate they saw Justice lift a hand, and the gate swung open. With

Amos on his saddlehorse, Hugh and Marguerite on the wagon seat, and the forlorn, black-eyed Candida in the rocker in the bed of the wagon, they rode forth, following the tall man on the Appaloosa horse onto the yellow-grass plains of Dakota Territory.

2

THERE WAS A cold wind blowing from out of the north, bending the long grass before it. A scattering of clouds moved across the high skies, their shadows flitting across the earth.

The Denton wagon rumbled along the cotton-wood-lined creekbed road, following the ruts, which were overgrown now with grass—the road had not been used much lately. Not by those who were now alive.

Ruff Justice rode off to the north of the wagon, his eyes scanning the grasslands, knowing that their empty appearance could be a deadly illusion. He had seen Sioux by the hundreds suddenly appear on seemingly empty prairie, and just now he wanted no such surprise.

He rode a fool's mission, and he knew it. The Dentons must have twisted the colonel's arm pretty hard to ever get the old man to agree to this. A Sunday drive through a battlefield.

But if a man could push those thoughts aside it was a beautiful day. The temperature was fifty or so, with the wind a bit chilling, but it was bracing. The clouds formed themselves into suggestions of sailing ships and castles, then dissipated, scudding away to the south.

The long grass was green, turning silver in the wind, and the Appy moved easily beneath Justice. A scattering of cottonwoods dotted the countryside, and here and there Justice saw a marmot den—piles of stones or jumbles of dead wood where the marmots went to hind legs, whistled, and ducked into their secret hiding places.

A fool's mission . . . maybe MacEnroe figured he had the right man for that kind of a job. Justice smiled, turning slightly in the saddle to glance back toward the Denton wagon.

Marguerite sat there small and pretty, wearing a blue bonnet to shade her face. Justice couldn't imagine anyone looking more out of place. She was cut for the ballrooms of Baltimore, an opera house. Not that there wasn't steel in her—her eyes flashed with it from time to time.

Her brother, that Hugh Denton, now he was a different matter. There was a cruelty lurking in his eyes, a bitterness in the set of his mouth. Amos—he seemed simply dull, brutal, completely under his brother's control.

These were just passing impressions, and Justice did not dwell on them. He could imagine what they thought of him.

The wind turned colder with each passing hour, and the clouds thickened. He would be wearing that buffalo coat he had in his roll before night fell.

It was late in the year for this. Damned late. Even the Sioux would be holing up soon—you can't make war when there is no graze for the ponies.

Far off to the west Justice could see a low purple line. Those were the Rockies, which had to be crossed before Camas. If it snowed they would not get through, it was that simple. Those folks in that wagon, could they imagine what a high-country winter was like, with the temperature plummeting forty degrees or more in an hour, with the wind howling up the long canyons?

It didn't matter—chances were damned slim they'd ever even reach the Rocky Mountains.

The shadows were lengthening, and Justice swung the Appaloosa's head toward the creek road, looking toward the evening meal. Their camp might as well be here as anywhere—there was no secure site for them on the Dakota plains.

"We can make another five miles!" Hugh Denton called from the wagon seat as Justice rode beside them.

"No sense hurrying, Mr. Denton," Ruff replied. "We'll only tire the horses."

There was no sense in hurrying at all. Disaster never cared what pace a man took. They were not outrunning the Sioux, could not hide from them or outfight them. There was no hurry at all.

Denton muttered something to Marguerite and slowed the team, letting the horses cool a little before they finally halted beside the creek, making camp in the purple dusk.

The river gurgled past, clear and fast. Justice walked to it, smelling the bacon frying, hearing the trace chains being dropped from the wagon.

He got to hands and knees and washed his face. The water was icy, biting, and the wind chilled his flesh. He ran hands across his dark hair and stood, hat in hand.

Marguerite was behind him, smiling, an errant curl across her high forehead.

"I needed water for coffee."

"You should be able to catch some before it all runs by," Justice said with the faintest of smiles. Dooley Dog, who had been trailing Justice by quite a bit, finally arrived, and he lay down near the creek to drink from a shallow pool, his sides rising and falling rapidly.

"Are you sure that's your dog?" Marguerite wanted to know. "You don't seem to tend him much."

"Dooley and I are friends," Justice said with a straight face. "Ours is not the common master and slave arrangement. He wanted to stop and pursue a marmot. I did not wish to."

Marguerite smiled, still trying to guess if Justice was serious or not. The sundown skies were spread deeply with orange and crimson clouds. These clouds had the aspect of threat to them, unlike the fluffy clouds they had seen throughout the day.

"Will it rain?" she asked, standing with her bucket of water.

"Seems likely," Ruff answered. He was watching as Commodore drank from the stream. Affectionately he patted the Appaloosa's shoulder. The shadows were deep under the cottonwoods, and when he glanced up he was surprised to find that Marguerite was still watching him. "Was there something you wanted?" he asked.

"No. Nothing just now," she answered. Then, swinging her bucket, she walked briskly past him, hoisting her skirt with one hand. Justice watched her go, recognizing what he saw—a very beautiful, very dangerous woman. Why he thought that, he could not have said. It was a sixth sense, he supposed. Those who have lived long on the frontier, in constant danger, have some such instinct, indefinable but strong, real.

That sort of sense which causes a man to take the left fork of the road, when the right was the more logical choice, only to find out later that the right led into trouble and death.

A sort of small bell rang in a man's head at such times. Whims, some called them, and they had the right to call them what they chose. But Ruff had learned long ago not to ignore this instinct.

Now that little bell was sounding as he watched the fluid hips of Marguerite Denton, her straight back and auburn curls. That little bell was ringing in his head, and a second bell a little lower.

She was a hell of a sensuous woman.

"You never have those problems, do you, Dooley Dog?" Justice asked.

Dooley cocked his head, and his stub of a tail wagged furiously. Justice put his hat back on and sniffed the air, looking once to the deeply shadowed hills beyond the camp. The sky still held an orange light.

"Let's get on up there. They're burning that bacon."

Justice led his Appy to the perimeter of the camp. The fire was blazing hotly against the dusk. It was enough campfire for forty men, and enough to be seen for forty miles.

Ruff walked to the fire and methodically kicked sand into it. Amos sat staring at him stupidly, and Hugh Denton came to his feet.

"What are you doing? It's getting cold. It'll be colder by morning."

"I mean to live to see morning," Justice said quietly. Then he sat, and by the light of the dully glowing embers he chewed on thickly sliced, smoky bacon.

Hugh Denton and his brother exchanged glances, but neither of them said anything. When Justice was through he dipped into the frying pan again, tossing the remaining bacon to Dooley Dog.

"It could be I wanted the rest of that," Amos Denton said in a low voice.

"Take it from him," Justice said and shrugged. Dooley Dog glanced up as if he understood and then went back to his munching.

"That's plain insulting," Amos Denton said. He drew back his coat flap, revealing the walnut butt of a Smith & Wesson.

"I guess you could say so," Justice agreed. He drew a handkerchief from his pocket and wiped his fingers and then his mouth and mustache.

"You think I wouldn't kill you?" Amos asked. He was a big man and now he stood, his chest rising and falling with anger.

"I think you'd be a fool to try it."

Amos peered across the embers at the tall man who was coolly folding his handkerchief. Justice's eyes suddenly came up to meet his own, and Amos flinched. There was a devil lurking in those eyes, and Amos felt a cold chill crawl up his spine.

Yet the big man couldn't help pushing it. "Think you could take me, do you?"

"I know it," Justice said solemnly. "If I didn't—well, the wild country would take care of you anyway. Without me."

"You think we're imbeciles, don't you?" Hugh Denton said.

"No," Justice said honestly. "I think you're smart enough to know what you're into. But you think you can handle it—I know you can't. I've seen the elephant, Denton, seen him and thrown him. You—you ain't seen his droppings. If you had, you'd have turned tail already."

"You think you're something, don't you?" Amos exploded.

Justice didn't respond to it. He turned, stroking Dooley's head. The dog's wide pink tongue dangled from its mouth.

"What is it you don't like about us?" Hugh Denton asked. The man's face was lean, glossed and shadowed by the light from the embers.

"I don't dislike you, sir," Justice said candidly. "But I don't like playing nursemaid to a pack of fools. Anyone who wanders this territory just now—experienced or not—is riding into the teeth of death."

"You afraid of dyin'?" Amos sneered.

"I am afraid of dying stupidly," Justice said frankly. Marguerite, who had been at the wagon tending to her sister, reappeared, and she glanced from Ruff to her brothers and back, reading the conflict in their expressions.

"How is she?" Justice asked.

"Fine. She had some appetite."

"Good. If you'll excuse me, then," Ruff said, rising, "I'll make my bed away from the camp."

He got to his feet, and Amos Denton felt his stomach sink a little. All the time Denton had been baiting the tall man, pushing him, Justice had had his Colt in his hand, or near it. In the darkness Amos had not seen it beside Ruff's leg. Now he did, and he swallowed hard.

Justice leveled a cold glance at Amos, and he said without intonation, "Sorry—it's only a habit."

They watched as Justice tipped his hat and shouldered his roll. He turned then and strode off into the shadows, Dooley Dog rising to follow him.

It was a minute before Marguerite spoke, and when she did her voice was low, throttled with emotion in the darkness. "You fools are going to ruin everything. That man is our only chance of getting through to Camas, and you"—she fixed a searing glare on Amos— "want to shoot him! Talk to him, Hugh. Talk to him and tell him how things lie."

She spun and stalked away toward the wagon, and

Amos hung his head, knowing she was right. Still, he could hardly stomach that fancy-dressing, smooth-talking scout. He rose and threw the dregs of his coffee against the embers, and steam rose against the cold air.

In the darkness Hugh said to him, "Don't worry, Amos. Justice is with us because we have the need for him. When we no longer have that need . . ." His voice fell away and mingled with the night's silence.

Justice had withdrawn a hundred yards from the camp of the Dentons, and he spread his roll beside a lightning-struck oak. Dooley lay silently beside him.

The clouds had smothered the stars, and the night was dark. The early-rising halfmoon had lost itself among the whey of the clouds and showed now only as a faintly silver glow.

Justice sat silently for a long while, his long arms wrapped around his knees, studying the dark outlines of the camp, the far reaches, the cold clouds.

These were odd folks he was traveling with. They had taken him on as scout, though not willingly. They needed him to survive this land; yet they obviously resented his presence. Why was that?

Did it have anything to do with the shadow of a woman named Candida? It was inexplicable to Justice that the Dentons should carry the obviously sick girl with them. There had been no one to leave the girl with, Marguerite said. Did that justify it?

"There's something no one wants to tell me, Dooley." The dog lifted one ear, listening.

Well, let them have their secret—whatever it was.

"Only thing is, dog, it's liable to be a secret that gets us killed."

It was midnight or near it when Justice was nuzzled into alertness by Dooley's cold nose. Ruff sat upright, his hand going automatically to the Spencer repeater, which lay beside his head.

Dooley was standing, his muzzle pointing toward the Denton camp, his body rigid, and Justice rested a hand on the dog's back.

"Where?" he asked, and then he saw it himself. A shadowy figure moved through the trees beyond the camp, and as Justice listened, he heard the faint, sand-muffled sounds of a horse walking away up the creekbed.

He got to his feet and moved silently down the draw toward the camp, circling slightly so as to come upon it from the south. The air was damp, chill, the scent of sage and buffalo grass heavy. Dooley moved silently ahead of Ruff.

Neither of them made a sound. Justice had lived too much among and around the Indians not to have learned himself how to move silently.

Quietly they moved into the river bottom, and Dooley, who had gone out ahead, circled and finally stopped, sitting on the coarse sand.

Justice went to where the dog waited, and, squatting, he found the sign. His fingers searched the sand, finding the indentations left by a horse's hooves. Then, by the dim light of the lurking moon, he saw a man's bootprints.

Not an Indian then—but who?

Who on this Sioux-infested prairie? There were suddenly a lot of people willing to risk a savage death to ride this country.

Justice eased up toward the camp, and halting in the wrought-iron shadows the cottonwoods cast he searched it with his eyes. No one moved, and Justice could see them in their beds.

Silence and stillness. Yet there was a lingering scent of dust in the cold air. Someone from the camp had moved down to the river bottom and spoken to the stranger.

By daylight he might be able to make more out of the tracks, but just now he had learned all that it was possible to learn. He withdrew into the trees, crossed the creek, and circled back to his bed on the knoll, his eyes alert to the darkness.

If there had been one, there might well be others.

Justice was uneasy as he rolled into his bed, but nevertheless he slept peacefully, knowing that Dooley was at hand and on watch.

Morning brought a gray dawn. Off to the northwest, rain was already falling, darkening the plains, and it looked as though the weather would catch them within an hour.

Justice walked to the Denton camp, where Hugh was just rolling out. They exchanged looks but said nothing. Marguerite was at the fire, wearing a man's hat and a man's coat over her dress. She offered Justice coffee, which he took, and as she handed it to him, she brushed against him. It was a definite, unspoken invitation, and Justice smiled faintly, studying her smooth face, those pursed lips which he would have bet were skilled in all of their many uses.

"Any coffee left, Marge?" Amos Denton asked, his expression surly. "Or did Justice give it to his dog?"

"There's plenty, Amos," Marguerite answered, an edge to her words.

"He thinks more of that damned dog than of people," Amos went on, speaking to Marguerite as if Justice were not even there.

"Perhaps I have good reason for that," Ruff said quietly. Marguerite smiled, and Amos scowled deeply. Justice turned and walked to the front of the wagon, where Hugh was harnessing his horses.

"They look some worn down already," Justice commented.

"They'll do," Denton muttered.

Justice shrugged and walked to the back of the wagon. Flipping the canvas back, he sat on the tailgate, sipping his coffee.

"That's quite a batch of relatives you've got there."

Candida did not answer, as she answered no comment. Her black eyes stared into the distances. Fixed neither on Justice nor on the lowering gray skies, but on some indeterminate point in between, nowhere. What was it she saw, what was it she looked for?

"There's coffee back yonder. I'd fetch some for you if you'd like it. It's not much really. I favor a little chicory in mine." He smiled at Candida, whose expression, an empty, lost expression, had not changed in the slightest. "But chicory is hard come by. There's wild chicory up higher in the mountains—it's got these pretty little blue flowers. I don't know if you've ever seen it. But I'll show it to you when we get to the Rockies—assuming it's not all covered with snow."

"What in hell are you doing, Justice?"

Hugh Denton was there, red-faced, trembling with anger.

"Talking to the girl is all. Everybody likes to talk to someone from time to time."

"Candida does not speak," he replied stiffly.

"I know. But I figured she wouldn't mind hearing a voice. Maybe she can't hear me at all," Justice added, looking at the beautiful, waxen dark-eyed girl. "But then—that couldn't bother her none, could it?"

Justice winked at Candida and slid from the tailgate, eyeing the threatening skies. The wind shook the leaves from the cottonwoods and laid the grass flat against the earth.

"Weather's comin' in hard, Denton. What do you want to do? Travel through it or sit it out?"

"What do you recommend?" Denton asked.

"Turning back, but since you won't do that, I suppose we might as well move on. If it gets too bad we can always stop."

The rain came in swiftly and hard. It was miserable and cold, but it did have an advantage—the Sioux were unlikely to be stirring, unlikely to spot them. Of course as heavy as this rain was they could ride right into the middle of an Oglala camp without ever seeing it.

Justice shouldered into his big buffalo coat, and he told Denton, "I'll stay closer than I have been. We'll take it slow. I'd hate to have the wagon roll into a creek we didn't see."

Denton shouted his understanding above the roar of the rain, and he clambered onto the wagon seat, wearing a dark slicker and a hat which streamed water. Marguerite was beside him, but now he realized suddenly that he hadn't seen Amos Denton for some time. Turning in his saddle, Ruff looked through the slanting rain in every direction, but he could not spot either Denton or the strapping sorrel he was riding.

Sudden thunder boomed across the plains, and the skies crackled with lightning, spinning eerie white webs of menace among the jumbled, storm-torn clouds.

The rain came in still harder, like a wall of water driving into their faces, as Justice led the small party out of the creekbed and toward the higher ground where there was less chance of flooding.

That creek road, like many another road, had been built on river bottom because it was the easiest route. Now, like all such trails, it would be washed away. Ruff lined the wagon westward by keeping the wind and rain on his right shoulder, then they moved out, the horses laboring through the rain.

Now they would move without great difficulty; but later, when the ground became saturated, muddy, those horses would have the devil's own time. They would need plenty of rest. That meant traveling slowly. Traveling slowly meant doubling the risk of meeting a Sioux war party, doubling the chance that those far Rocky Mountain passes would be blocked by snow.

The Dentons should have purchased oxen, not horses, for their team, but they were greeners, and apparently no one told them. Now they would have to make do.

Ruff rode slowly through the storm, fighting against the wind, his eyes peppered with cold rain as he tried to find a trail over and through the washes, which were already running water.

Twice they were cut off and had to backtrack nearly a mile. When it happened again Denton was furious.

"I'll be damned! I'll take this rig through."

The water was rushing down the wash before them, nearly three feet deep and moving with speed. An uprooted tree bobbed past, showing momentarily through the churning white water.

"That makes about as much sense as pulling your rig in front of a locomotive, Denton!" Justice hollered above the roar of the water, the howl of the wind.

"I can make it," Denton shouted. Rainwater ran in rivulets from his lean face.

"You'll make it to Nebraska—and fast, if you try that stunt. Or to hell," Ruff said.

Denton was hearing no argument, and for a minute Justice thought the man was actually going to try it, but the undercut bank before them suddenly caved in and was instantly washed away, staining the water brown for a moment. That seemed to wash away Denton's resolve as well, and he nodded slowly as Marguerite imploringly clutched at his sleeve.

Justice turned the Appy and rode slowly southward, and when he glanced back through the steel curtain of the storm Denton was following.

They forded near Canyon Creek just at the mouth of Cable Canyon and moved only another half mile or so westward before darkness and rain made traveling any more that day impossible. They camped along Cable Canyon with only four miles gained that day.

Denton's horses were exhausted, and Justice mentioned it.

"They look fine to me," Hugh snapped. "Just why in hell are you trying to slow us down, Justice?"

Ruff glanced skyward, where a thundering explosion shook the heavens. "It's God slowin' you, Denton, not me. Maybe you know why that might be."

Then he turned and walked toward the wind-whipped fire Marguerite had managed to start in a hollow along the canyon wall. The wind was somewhat stilled in the canyon, but the flutes and hollows along the canyon sides caused it to shriek and moan eerily.

There was no escaping the rain. It battered the rust-red canyon walls and flowed over rocks and through chutes and funnels toward the river which raged below.

Close against the wall, however, it was drier, and next to the fire which glowed in the hollow, it was warm enough to get by.

There was just enough room in that hollow for the wagon and team, and so at least Candida would be out of the weather. Amos, who had finally reappeared with some lame explanation of having been off riding south flank, hunkered over a cup of coffee, his dark eyes on Justice.

Ruff was wet and cold, as they all were, and he was in no mood for arguing with the Dentons, so he kept his mouth shut except to ask Marguerite, "Wouldn't it be a good idea to get that girl down from the wagon from time to time, let her move her legs?"

"She's perfectly all right," Marguerite answered breezily.

Justice shrugged and sipped at his coffee, sawing off slices from one of the hams as he drank. He tossed them into the black skillet over the fire, and they hissed pleasantly, the smoky smell of the frying ham reaching their nostrils enticingly for a moment before it was lost in the windswept night.

Marguerite had broken out the beans again, and she spooned some beside Justice's ham, her eyes meeting his warmly. Amos and Hugh had given up talking altogether.

They sat close together, their rifles across their laps, shoveling food into their mouths. The rain ran off their hats and shoulders, and Amos trembled slightly with the cold.

Lightning arced across the canyon, and the darkness went briefly as light as day. The cold trees were glossed with silver, shaking violently in the wind; the creek, swollen with the inrushing freshets, boiled over the rocky streambed.

Then the lightning stilled and the world went dark with only the following rumble of heavy thunder sounding above the roar of the rain.

"Damn—it's comin' in harder again," Amos grumbled, his rubbery mouth set in an expression of nearly animal dismay.

He was right. It hit them like a wall of water, the

cold downpour erasing all sights and sounds. It drowned the fire as it gusted into the hollow and pelted them like silver buckshot, roaring down the long dark canyon.

Ruffin gave it up. Putting down his plate, he snatched up his rifle and moved back into the hollow, his roll over his shoulder.

The Dentons had made a dash for the wagon at the same time, and that was dry enough. But Ruff had no wish to spend the night so near to those two.

He was pulled back to the wall of the hollow, the rain washing around him. Peering against the storm, he now saw, by the flash of distant lightning, a narrow crevice above his head which led back into another higher, shallower hollow.

Ruff tossed his rifle up and climbed onto the ledge, walking through the rain to the back wall of the second cove. There was an overhang, and there was room for a bed. Clearing away some rocks and old debris, Ruff spread out his roll.

Again brilliant lightning flashed—a bone-white ladder of chain lightning illuminating the rolling skies. The canyon was awash with water; Justice could see the black water roaring from all the tributaries along Cable Canyon.

The wind still howled, the rain still fell. But here, in this tiny hollow, it was nearly dry, nearly windless. Ruff spread his groundsheet and laid out his buffalo coat, which was as warm a blanket as a man could wish for. Then he settled down and took off his belt and hat.

The lightning flashed again, and Ruff saw a sight that stood his hair on end.

Automatically his hand tightened on the receiver of his Spencer carbine. The lightning flashed and flared again. Justice watched them wind their way along the river bottom.

Sioux. There were at least fifty of them, walking their ponies through the cold darkness, like savage ghosts. He watched them, every nerve in his body alert.

They were on the far side of the river, and probably would not cross it without reason. Had they a reason? That fire had been dangerous. That smoke, even the smell of frying ham, could be picked up a mile away—if not for the wind and the rain.

Perhaps this storm they had cursed was all that was saving them. The Indians, shoulders hunched against the weather, heads bowed, wound through the willows and continued southward. Behind them trailed a dozen captured army horses.

Then they were gone, and the night closed in again, but Justice remained where he was, watching the canyon through the silver screen of the rain which dripped from the overhang.

"Keep on riding, damn you," he whispered. He did not want them in the canyon at dawning. He whispered his wish a second time. It was like wishing death away, but perhaps this time, somehow, it would work.

The Sioux would logically hole up in the canyon, where the weather would be cut some, but perhaps they had to be somewhere else at sunrise—at some meeting point, some battlefield. There was no telling. But for now they were gone, and the rain and the darkness which had been cause for grumbling now seemed close allies.

Justice rolled back against the back wall of the hollow once more, propping his rifle up beside him, and he drew the buffalo coat up over him, closing his eyes.

It was Dooley again who awakened him, and with a start Justice sat up, drawing back the massive curved hammer of the Spencer. A shadow loomed up and moved toward him, and Dooley crouched low.

"I didn't think I'd be able to find you," Marguerite said. The wind whipped at her loose wrapper. Her hair drifted free in dark profusion against the lightning-bright skies, and she slipped in beside him, her wrapper falling to the floor of the hollow.

3

⬩⬩⬩⬩ ◆➤ ◆ ◆ ⬩⬩⬩⬩

THE NIGHT WAS cold, but she was warm. The rain drove down outside, but within the tiny hollow it was dry, cozy. Justice lifted his buffalo coat, and Marguerite slipped into his bed, clinging to him, her mouth searching his.

Lightning flashed, and by that light Ruff saw her smooth bare shoulders, her eager face, lovely full breasts which his hands found and stroked, searching minutely before he drew her to him again, holding her close beneath the heavy coat.

"Hell of a way to wander around out here—there were Sioux out there," he told her.

She kissed his throat, his mustached lip. "Will they be back?"

"Who knows?"

"Either way—I made the right decision," Marguerite decided. "If they come back, this is the safest place to be. And if worst comes to worst, I won't have to die alone in that cold."

Justice couldn't argue with her logic, nor did he wish to. She was warm against him, and he shed his buckskins like a snake shedding its skin. It was cold as he sat up to pull off his shirt, but only for a moment.

Marguerite was all over him as he lay back down,

her fingers going directly to his cock, which was throbbing, lengthening in response to her touch.

Ruff drew her to him, his hand clenching her smooth, cool buttocks, feeling the silky flesh of her full hips. He felt her mouth against his, warm and soft, and he took her tongue hungrily into his own mouth.

"It's not so cold out here," Marguerite decided. She leaned her head forward, and her teeth bit into his shoulder as her hand massaged his shaft, which was now fully erect, ready.

"You're a big man," Marguerite sighed into his ear as she continued to search his erection, nearly frantically. "I knew you would be. . . . Do you like that? Do you like the way I touch it, Ruff? Is it right?"

"What do you think?" His hands ran along her hips and thighs. She was pressed against him now, her breasts flattened against his hard chest.

"I can make you feel better," she promised. Lightning crackled again, and by that light Justice saw her face. Her eyes were wide with excitement. Her dark hair flowed across her shoulders, down her smooth white back. She licked her lips hungrily and rolled to Justice, lifting her trembling leg high as she straddled him, her warm cleft meeting the underside of his shaft. An electrical current to match the waves of lightning surged up in Ruff's loins.

Her teeth chattered with the cold as Marguerite sat straight up, and as the buffalo coat fell aside, Justice felt the gusts of chilling wind himself. But astride him she lifted herself higher, and he felt a point of heat caress the head of his cock as she touched him to her inner flesh, her fingers running crazily over him there.

Justice's own fingers went to meet hers, and they joined, easing his thick length into Marguerite. Now again she shuddered violently, but it was not with the cold, but with the thrill of excitement which crawled over and through her. Her head was thrown back and lightning tore the skies outside apart, illuminating her face, which was tight with concentration. Her eyes flashed with the brilliant white light; her flesh was an eerie blue-white. Her breasts jutted out proudly as she settled onto Ruff's swollen shaft, as the thunder rumbled up the canyons and he clutched at her, grabbing her fine white shoulders, pulling her to him, smothering her with his kiss as the pulse within him rose to a drumming need.

Marguerite went to him, her mouth meeting his in a slow, demanding kiss as her hips rose and settled against Justice, then rose again, her body fluid and warm as he held her.

The rain drove down, and Justice drew the buffalo coat around them, wrapping them in a warm, passionate cocoon where the cold could not touch them, nor the wind, nor the rain.

Marguerite swayed against Justice, and her warmth trickled down as she quivered, impaling herself on his erection. Whispering constantly into his ear, she rode him wildly.

"Do that again. Can you feel that?" she breathed into Justice's ear, her hands running down his thighs, up to his lips. Her mouth was open against his ear, and she swayed, methodically, her throat issuing tiny, pleasurable moans which were followed by deliberate, probing movements of her pelvis, which she ground against Justice.

"Lord, it's big. I'm full," she breathed, and her whispers, her tiny touches, brought Justice's own need to a higher peak. Slowly now he began to arch his back, to thrust against her, to feel himself slipping into her warm depths as she rode him, encouraging him, her fingers searching everywhere.

"Yes. Higher. Mm . . . now you're doing it to me!" Marguerite breathed, and she grew tense, her mouth finding Justice's chest as she held perfectly still for a moment, letting Justice drive into her, send that electricity through her body.

"No more. Yes. More!" she shouted against the night, and Justice felt her come undone inside, felt the hot flow of her need, her orgasm, and she wriggled against him like a fish on a line, her hands clutching his cock, gripping his buttocks as he arched his back more, the need building in him until he could hold it back no longer and he held Marguerite to him, his hands spreading her wider, dipping into her as his climax filled her.

Then it was still. It was warm beneath the buffalo coat, and she was a woman, warm and soft within the cold night. The rain poured down and the wind rumbled, but they paid it no mind, they gave no thought to the Sioux, but only to each other as their hearts stilled.

She was warm, and her lips, which continued to search Justice, were soft. He closed his eyes and listened to the rain, feeling her against him.

He felt Marguerite slip away from him, and he opened an eye, seeing dawn break through the scattered clouds along the horizon. Red arrows of morning flashed against the darker skies. A line of pure beaten gold lay along the dark horizon.

The rains had stopped; it would be clear traveling that day. Justice slipped from his bed and, shivering in the chill of morning, stepped into his buckskins, drawing his hair back with his fingers before planting his wide-brimmed hat. Then he rolled up his bedding.

"Up, Dooley! It's breakfast time."

The little dog sprang to its feet and followed Ruff as he slid from the hollow down the damp red chute below, into the main camp where Hugh Denton was only now rising, although it seemed Amos had been up for some time.

Marguerite was at the fire, and she turned her head, an utterly feminine smile on her broad mouth. Her eyes were deep and soft as they met those of Ruff Justice, but she said nothing.

He crouched near the fire, Dooley beside him, his rifle in his hand, watching as the coffee boiled. From time to time he let his eyes go to the plains beyond, searching the flat grasslands. He saw nothing, but he did not doubt the Sioux were out there.

Apparently they had been traveling to a meeting place. Otherwise they would have taken refuge against the storm. If they had traveled on through the night, as it appeared they had, then they would now be many miles away and there was little to fear.

From that band. Suppose other bands of warriors were trailing them, all funneling through Cable Canyon en route to a rendezvous?

Justice spoke none of his thoughts to the others, but he realized they would be in danger for quite a while yet, and the sooner they were away from Cable Canyon, the better.

Justice ate quickly, quietly, and when he was through, he told Hugh Denton, "Let's get it rolling, Denton. North for a ways."

"North! I heard the road followed Cable Canyon for a good ten miles."

"Mr. Justice thinks there are Sioux around," Marguerite put in. "We saw them last night."

"Sioux? Here?" Denton was unbelieving. He glanced around as if evidence of their passing could still be found. "I don't believe it. I'd've seen them, heard them."

"That's just the trouble, Mr. Denton—you won't see

them or hear them until it's too late. And if we follow Cable any longer, I'm afraid we will see them, for the last time."

Then he tugged his hat low and saddled Commodore, brushing the water from his black-and-silver saddle as he threw it on the Appy's back.

Slowly he walked around Commodore as he did each morning, searching for any infirmity, a thorn which might have been picked up unnoticed and which now would be festering, a scrape or bruise. He lifted each hoof in turn, checking for stones or loose shoes, then, satisfied, he stepped into leather, turning the horse sharply toward the north.

Commodore was feeling spry on this morning, and so Ruff let him run for a ways, Dooley sprinting after them. Then he halted, on a hillrise, and he looked down the long backtrail, watching as the Denton wagon followed, struggling through the mud, which was deep in the river bottom.

He peered eastward then, into the following sun, searching for the Sioux, for smoke or a patch of color, and for the lone rider who was still following them.

The going was slower now. Twice the wagon had bogged down and Amos and Justice had had to tie on with their horses before it was pulled free of the mire.

The day was clear, but colder yet, and with each hour the imposing bulk of the Rockies grew larger. They camped that evening near a grove of oaks where a spring bubbled up from out of solid stone and trickled away toward the Tongue River.

Justice knew this area well, knew that the spring was sacred to the Crow. Once he and Four Dove had camped here . . . before war had come to the plains, and the Crow, the immemorial enemy of the Sioux, had withdrawn to the west. Not to avoid fighting the Sioux, which they had always done, but to avoid becoming embroiled in the war with the whites.

Quail called from the low brush along the narrow stream as daylight faded to purple dusk and the shadows met and blended together. Justice had rubbed down Commodore, picketed him where there was good graze, and had washed in the spring where it issued from the gray granite.

The fire was burning, but the Dentons were all off somewhere when Justice settled beside it. He saw Marguerite leading a shaky Candida toward the stream, moving through the deep shadows of the oaks. Marguerite lifted a hand to Justice, but it was the other woman who held his thoughts for a moment.

A sad, shy thing, Candida. Her heart torn from her by the shock of her father's death. Was it such a good idea to take her to where it had actually happened, to collect Major Denton's remains and place them in the wagon, beside Candida?

Justice shook his head—it was their decision; he was only following orders.

He tested the coffee pot, found that it was hot, and poured himself a cup as evening settled in. Dooley lay in the tall grass, his head between his paws.

Ruff slipped his journal from his saddlebags, and, propping himself up against a decaying log, he scribbled in it with the stub of a pencil he carried.

"Writing a record of our journey?" Marguerite asked. She stood over him, holding Candida's hand. Candida looked as if she would like to dart away, to hide from this tall man, but she remained immobile as Ruff rose, smiling at them.

"I was writing a poem," Justice replied. Candida's dark eyes seemed to focus briefly, and Ruff touched her dark hair with the back of his hand. "I'm writing a poem to you, Candida, and when I am through, I shall read it to you."

Just for a moment her eyes seemed to reflect understanding, and then the light went out. Justice stepped back and watched as Marguerite led the pale, silent girl back to the wagon.

It was already too dark for writing, and so Ruff stuffed the journal book back into his pack. Amos had come in from out of the shadows, and he sat on a rock opposite Justice, the fire flickering between them.

"A poem," Denton said disgustedly. "Did you say you are writing a poem, Justice? Is that what you are—some kind of poet? Hell, I thought you was a rough-and-tumble plainsman."

"A little of each, I should say," Ruff answered mildly.

Marguerite had returned, and she poured herself a cup of coffee, sitting beside her brother.

"I didn't know you were something of a poet, Ruff," she said.

"Something of one." He nodded. "Folks have been known to sit still and listen to me . . . long as I have my gun out. Even spoke once in Kensington Hall."

"What's that?" Amos grumbled.

Justice glanced sharply at the man, his coffee cup frozen in midair.

"It's an opera house . . . in Baltimore," Justice said.

"You know, Amos," Marguerite prompted, "Kensington is where Buffalo Bill's western show used to play."

"I forgot," Amos said. He lifted his eyes and found those of Justice on him across the fire. "I never did get down that way much."

"You . . . read down at the Kensington, did you?"

Marguerite asked hurriedly. She smoothed her skirt out, avoiding Justice's eyes.

"Yeah. Once. I swung through with Bill Cody. It didn't seem they cared much for my reading, though." He shrugged.

"Well, there's no accounting for tastes."

Marguerite attempted a quick smile, but it was most unconvincing. She changed the subject.

"What is that on your dog's collar—that silver plate? I noticed it back at Abraham Lincoln."

"A little something Alexander Pope wrote—doggerel, if you'll allow me the expression." Justice smiled thinly. He stroked Dooley's head affectionately. "A little reminder for me. . . . It says," he quoted, " 'I am his Highness' dog at Kew; Pray tell me, sir, whose dog are you?' "

"Meanin'?" Amos asked sourly.

"Meaning," Justice answered as he stretched, "that this is a highborn dog. A king's dog, the best." He scratched Dooley's ear. "Now that's fine for Dooley, for any dog—it means he's worth something. As for me," Ruff went on, leaning far forward so that the firelight glossed his face, "I am no man's dog. It don't matter who—king, emperor, saint. It's *not* fitting for a man."

"Don't make no damned sense," Amos groused. "Never heard of anyone puttin' such on a mutt's collar."

"Mutt! As I said, sir, Dooley is a highborn dog."

"There's something else on that collar," Marguerite put in. "Two silver baubles. What are they?"

"These?" Ruff turned back Dooley's hair and showed them the two silver trinkets. "Those are Dooley's coup sticks."

Amos laughed out loud and waved a hand. Marguerite frowned, looking from one man to the other. "I don't understand."

"It's this way," Ruff told her. "An Indian will kill his enemy. But the bravest of the Indian warriors used to sneak up on an enemy and touch him with a stick they carried—called a coup stick. Now to do that, unarmed, was counted as a whole lot braver than shooting a man down.

"On long winter nights the men sit around telling tales of bravery. The things they've done. Counting coup, they call it."

"I've heard the expression," Marguerite said. She was leaning forward, her arms around her knees, fascinated.

Amos was less impressed. "And this little mutt does that, does he? Quite a trick, ain't it, Justice?"

"Dooley is not quite so skilled," Justice answered with a slow smile. "Each of these two sticks represents a time he has saved my life—but as you have suggested, he does not carry a stick, and he is not so gentle.

"Both of his victims are now dead. Both jugular cases."

Ruff looked up at Marguerite, whose face was immobile, and at Amos, who was trying to wear a scoffing expression but not quite managing it. The thing was, looking at that lean face of Ruff Justice over the firelight, Amos Denton knew the man was not lying, and he glanced apprehensively now at the small white dog beside him.

"I'll be making up my bed now," Ruff said, standing. "Good night, Marguerite." He bowed and hefted his roll, slipping off into the darkness, a squat white shadow behind him.

Marguerite waited a little while until the man was gone, and then she turned to Amos. "You idiot!" she exploded. "From Baltimore and never heard of the

Kensington! You blessed idiot. He's not a stupid man, this scout of ours, and he knows now, doesn't he, that you've never even been to Baltimore!"

"So what?" Amos grumbled. "He can't make nothin' out of it."

"No. Perhaps not. But I wouldn't bet on it, brother Amos. I certainly wouldn't put any money on it."

Justice rolled out his bed on a grassless knoll, then, as he habitually did, he searched the empty land, watching as the rising pale moon slowly illuminated the plains.

He could see Hugh Denton now, circling wide on his brother's horse—the Denton brothers had been taking turns riding watch, something Ruff considered totally useless. The Sioux, in numbers, could come up on their camp before either of them could get his mouth open. Even if they were able to sound a warning, what good would it do? The three of them and the two women against the Sioux nation.

But perhaps Hugh and Amos were not keeping their lookout for the Sioux. What then?

Justice frowned and watched as Hugh slowly dipped into a wash, was lost to the shadows, and re-emerged into the moonlight on the far side.

There was no reading this outfit. He thought of Amos Denton. The man, Ruff was sure, had never been to Baltimore. In fact his accent was more like Missouri than Maryland. Nor did he look much like Hugh—but then brothers don't always.

He wondered too about Marguerite. The way she had come to him out of the night—had that been her own notion? It seemed unlikely that it could have been any other way, but it gave a man cause to wonder.

If she had been sent to distract him, she had done a hell of a job. Justice lay back smiling as he recalled it.

He watched the stars for a long while, tugging up his
coat against the cold of the still night. Then he slept.

There was a row of red flowers along the hillrise,
and Justice picked them off one by one, the last one
exploding in a ball of flame . . . then he was riding
for all he was worth across an empty plain. The horse
plunged into the canyon and he fell with it, watching
their mocking faces.

Then he was drifting, drifting down the bloody
river, and he knew that only the woman could save
him. She smiled, beckoned, and he caught her hand
. . . but it came loose, blood streaming from the
wound as the woman's beautiful face turned to a
scab-ridden mummy's face. . . .

Justice sat bolt upright in his bed, his face dripping
sweat. The night was cold, still. Hours had passed,
and the moon was a high, silver globe against a star-
flecked sky.

That damned dream. Justice took a deep breath.

Standing, he faced the night. The empty plains, the
far mountains, the dark skies. You would think a man
could lose a dream like that out here. . . .

He tried to remember when it had started. Kiowa
Corners after the massacre? No, he had dreamed it
during the war at Chancellorsville. That morning he
had awakened to find Billy Short asleep in his arms—
his head blown away. And before that? Ruff could
not recall, as he never could.

He took his journal book from his pack, knowing
he would not sleep again that night. And by the scant
moonlight he scribbled his poem to Candida.

It was Justice who started the fire that morning and
ate a can of peaches while the coffee boiled and the
others climbed stiffly from their beds.

A low fog had drifted off the river, and it wound

through the trees, chilling their bones. When Marguerite had dressed and walked to the river to wash, Justice poured a cup of coffee and took it to the Denton wagon.

Throwing back the flap, he found Candida awake, already rocking in her chair, her eyes, as always, distant, empty. Justice leaned against the side of the wagon and offered her coffee.

"Still don't have any chicory to add to it, and I've been told I make it a mite strong, but it'll warm you some."

Candida rocked away, her hands resting inertly on her lap like two disabled white birds. Justice sipped his coffee and watched the sun cut through the fog, watched the birds take to wing across the morning skies.

"That's a pretty sight," he said quietly. "I favor the mornings. A lot of men like the night—but there's nothing about but men and night creatures. No, I like morning. Seeing nature come awake and stretch her muscles."

Candida did not answer, and Ruff stood, turning away. "They tell me you can't hear me. That I'm wasting my time. I don't believe it, Candida. You hear me? I know you've been hurt and you're hiding—I know about hiding. But you've got to beat it, girl. Fight off the night."

He nodded. "I'll be back. The poem's coming along."

Walking to the fire, he returned his cup without speaking to Hugh Denton, who sat there, scowling. Then Justice saddled Commodore and swung a long leg up and over.

"Due west," he told Hugh Denton, who glowered at him. Then, tugging his hat lower, Justice rode slowly out. While still in sight of the camp, Ruff reached back, withdrew a book from his saddlebags, and, hooking a knee around the pommel, rode westward, letting the Appy find its way while he read his Longfellow.

"Damn him," Hugh Denton breathed. "He's still snooping around Candida."

Amos had his hands thrust deeply into the pockets of his greasy coat. "Look at him," he muttered. "Ridin' the plains, spoutin' his poetry. I don't believe the tales I heard of this man, Hugh. I just don't believe he's that damned tough."

"We may have to find out one day," Hugh answered. He lifted his dark eyes, and from beneath his thick eyebrows, Amos watched back. Slowly the big man nodded and turned away, and Hugh repeated to himself, "We just may have to find out how tough this man is."

4

THE DAYS HELD clear as the small party reached the Yellowstone River, not fifty miles north of the Little Bighorn. The land was rolling hills with an occasional stand of oaks and cottonwood scattered along the river bottoms.

The supplies were holding out, which Justice was happy to see. He had no inclination to fire a weapon for any reason in this area, although it was rumored that the warring tribes had drifted north and east. A rumor in this country just wasn't good enough, however.

They held to their course. The Rockies grew larger with each morning until they dominated all of the world with their mass, their stark purple silhouette. The land was empty—outside of a small herd of buffalo they had seen nothing, no one for four days, and Ruff prayed that they would see no one.

The horses pulling the Denton wagon were done in, as Justice had foreseen. But there was no stopping to rest them. At his insistence Amos rotated his saddle bronc with the team. All that did was delay the inevitable; there were now three weary horses.

"They're in no shape for pulling the mountains," Ruff told Denton.

"Then, dammit, let's rest them," Hugh fired back angrily. Who he was angry at perhaps even Denton didn't know. His plans, seeming so simple in imagination, back in comfortable Baltimore, were sagging here on the broad plains.

"You know we can't stop," Ruff reminded him. His eyes searched the long hills. "Not out here."

"Then we'll drive them . . . till they die. Then we'll walk."

"Most likely," Justice agreed. The wind caught the brim of his hat, turning it back. "I may have an idea on where we can get some horses. Meanwhile," he told Denton, "I'll get on ahead, making sure we've got water and grass for the horses we have got."

Justice spun the Appaloosa then and rode into the wind. The breeze stirred the buckskin fringes of his jacket and leggings, and his dark curls flowed out behind him as he rode the grasslands, the dog panting along behind him.

"Look at that son of a bitch," Hugh said disgustedly. "Not a worry in the world. I think he's crazy!" Sweat trickled down Denton's forehead, stinging his eyes as he squinted into the sun.

"No." Marguerite smiled wistfully as her brother clambered into the box of the wagon. "It's not that— he's not crazy. Maybe to live out here a man has to be like Justice is. Able to shrug it all off, to put the Sioux, the snows, the mountains totally out of his mind. Of course," she said, turning her eyes to those of Hugh, "you could be right . . . he could be as crazy as they come."

"I don't like the way you smile when you talk about that man, Marge." Denton snapped the reins, and the exhausted team stumbled forward, the wagon creaking beneath them. "You aren't really beginning to fall for him, are you?"

"I don't know." Marguerite smiled again, her eyes following the dust the plainsman trailed into the crystal skies as he rode. She shrugged. "He's different from any man I've known. He doesn't play up to me. He doesn't brag, or even try to prove how strong and masculine he is. He just is. It's obvious. He oozes masculinity."

"He's good at sex," Hugh said sourly.

"That too," Marguerite agreed. She repeated it quietly. "That too, brother."

Hugh swallowed a bitter remark and settled to his driving, watching the long, empty land. Justice was out of sight now, as was Amos, who was trailing the wagon. There was nothing but the creaking of the wagon wheels, the infernal sounds of that strapped-down rocker in the bed of the wagon, the chill of the wind and the dust rising from the horses' hoofs.

Suddenly he was there, sitting a paint pony atop the knoll. Hugh grabbed for his rifle and pulled up the team, watching as the Indian, hand raised, walked his horse down toward the Denton wagon.

"What does he want?" Marguerite asked, clutching her brother's sleeve. Hugh shook her off, wanting his hands free.

He was a young Indian, no more than twenty-five, and he led a string of four horses. Hugh stepped down, standing beside the wagon as the brave approached, his hand still held high. He appeared to be unarmed but for a hunting knife.

Where was that damned Justice—now that they needed him? The Indian slid from his pony's back and walked around Denton's team, eyeing them expertly.

Amos was coming at a gallop from the south, and he hit the camp with his rifle in hand. The Indian simply glanced at him, and Hugh shook his head.

"You didn't see any others out there?" Hugh whispered.

"No. Just this one."

"Justice?"

Amos shrugged. He hadn't seen the tall man all morning. The Indian walked to where Hugh stood, and he shook his head. "Your ponies no good."

"They have come far," Hugh answered. His eyes still searched the horizon, alert for other movement. This man was not an Oglala, of that Denton was certain. Back at Fort Rice they had several Oglala Sioux prisoner, and this man was not dressed like them, nor did he facially resemble the Oglala.

"I trade you fresh ponies," the brave announced. "You will give me rifle too." He made a scooping motion with his fingers. "Some food."

"What do you think, Amos?"

Amos looked at the Indian, the weary team, the fresh ponies in turn. "Sounds fair to me," Amos replied. "We need fresh horses bad. I can give him that old Sharps buffalo gun. Throw in one of Justice's hams."

"I will trade," Hugh said. Then they dickered a bit, Hugh holding back some ammunition and the ham, finally giving in. The Indian took the rifle with satisfaction, helped Hugh switch teams, and then he trailed out, the ham slung over his shoulder.

The brave was a hundred yards off when they saw the dust. It was Justice, and he was coming on the run, that Appaloosa's mane and tail flying as he whipped its flanks with his hat.

The Indian glanced up, and then he dug his heels into his pony's ribs, dropping the lead to his string. He leaped that paint over a wash and lay across the withers, riding for all he was worth.

But that Appy hadn't been outrun yet, and as the

Indian raced through the tall grass, he caught sight of Justice closing fast. He drew up, spun the paint around, and brought the muzzle of that big Sharps .50 up.

It was too late. Justice hurled himself from the saddle and hit the Indian with a shoulder, the rifle exploding into the air. The two men tumbled to the earth as the paint pony reared up and galloped off.

The jolt slammed the breath from Ruff, but his head was clear. He scrambled to his feet, but the Indian was quicker. The brave was crouched, his knife in his hand, blade side up, for a disemboweling slash.

Ruff's hand went to his belt, and he brought his big stag-handled bowie out in one easy movement. He circled the Indian, his eyes glittering, alert.

The Indian was suddenly wary. This long-haired plainsman was no pilgrim. By his dress he had been much among the Indians, much upon the plains. And no man who is not a fighter has been much upon the Dakota plains.

But the brave had fought Crow, Cheyenne, Arapaho—the best fighters of his time and place—and he had no fear, only a healthy caution.

He feinted, taking a half-step forward, but Justice did not take the feint. Instead the plainsman stepped aside and kicked out, trying to take the brave's feet from under him, but the Indian was too quick for that.

They circled in the long grass, the sun hot on their backs. The warrior tried to step in, and his blade slashed upward, inches from Ruff's belly, narrowly missing his chin as it flashed past.

Ruff's forearm shot up and he blocked a second, downward stroke, his hand locking on the Indian's wrist. The Indian wriggled and brought a knee up hard, trying for Ruff's groin, but Justice was able to cross his own knee over and block the move. But the warrior slipped from his grip.

They were near together now, and Ruff's eyes locked with the black eyes of the Indian, seeing cool resolve in them, an animal confidence.

Ruff stepped in, swiped with his bowie, and withdrew quickly as the Indian countered with his own stroke. Now a thin line of red across the brave's hard copper abdomen trickled blood, and there was anger in the Indian's eyes for the first time.

He stepped in, and Ruff stepped aside, tripping and throwing the brave, who rolled to the grass. Justice threw himself at the brave, but he rolled aside and Ruff missed with a savage downthrust of his bowie.

The Indian was cat-quick and was on top of Ruff before he could get to his feet again. His knife arced through the air, but Ruff rolled his head aside, at the same time kicking up with both knees, and the warrior flew over Ruff's head, landing with a thud on his back.

Justice was up again, and so was the Indian. They circled warily now, each man knowing he had a fighter opposite him. The Indian came in, and they locked together, the scent of his body in Ruff's nostrils, the blood from his wound smearing against Justice's white elkskins.

Ruff held the Indian's knife hand locked to his side, and over the brave's head he held his bowie, the Indian's hand locked to his wrist. Slowly it came down, and the Indian watched it, seeing the sunlight glisten on the long, murderous blade.

Justice had the leverage on the man, and he brought it inexorably down. He gave a last violent thrust and the blade drove down, entering the warrior's throat at the collarbone.

He wriggled on the blade, bellowed a violent,

blood-choked curse, and then went limp. As Justice watched, the man sagged to the earth, life streaming from him, his knife falling uselessly to the earth, where it lay sparkling in the tall yellow grass.

Ruff stood over him, panting, the dust still swirling, getting into his nostrils. From the corner of his eye he could see the Dentons approaching, see Marguerite's eyes on him.

Then, taking a deep breath, Ruff got to one knee. He lifted the Indian's head by the hair and with a stroke of that razor-sharp bowie he took the warrior's scalp.

He stood holding the grisly trophy as Amos and Hugh came rushing up the knoll, leaving Marguerite to stand beside the wagon.

"Why did you kill him? Why?" Hugh screamed. "He's not Oglala—we just made a horse trade, that's all!"

Ruffin T. Justice turned to Denton, and in his eyes was the residual savagery of the fight. He let those eyes rest on Denton's face for a long minute before he spoke, his voice taut but soft.

"No, he wasn't Oglala. He was Lakota. Teton Lakota. Their chief's a man named Crazy Horse. You might have heard of him. They're allies to the Oglala.

"You made more than a horse trade here, Denton. You gave this man a gun. But that's not what he really wanted, either. He came down counting heads, wanting to see how well we were armed. He would have been back with his friends, Hugh. Then you would have found out how damned poor a bargain you made."

Justice was silent. The long hills ran away to the mountains, and he looked at them, never glancing at the dead man at his feet. The wind blew his hair, cooled his battle-warmed flesh.

He picked up his hat, dusted it, and planted it on his head.

"You scalped him!"

Justice turned to see Marguerite standing there, her hands to her mouth, her eyes wide. Ruff nodded.

"I want them to respect me," he said, returning his gaze to the golden, distant hills. "They must respect me—and fear me a little. They won't respect a warrior who would not take a scalp."

"It's savage. Pagan. Barbaric!" Marguerite said, her voice trembling.

"It's the killing which is barbaric," Ruff answered quietly. "After that has been done . . . what does the scalp matter?"

As they watched, he turned and went to where the ham lay in the grass. He picked it up, wiped it clean with his hand, and returned to Commodore, who waited patiently. Ruff swung into the saddle without glancing at them again. Then he swung the Appy's head around and rode slowly down the long hill, the wind in his hair.

"The son of a bitch," Hugh Denton said softly. There was mingled admiration, disgust, and awe in his curse. No one else said a thing. Together they walked back to the wagon, watching as Justice rounded up the Indian's string of horses.

They camped on a treeless knoll, and Justice did not complain about the campfire on this evening. They were to the western fringes of the Sioux territory, and despite the appearance of the lone Lakota, Justice felt somewhat secure. The rain a few days earlier had erased their tracks as far as Cable Canyon, and since then they had moved into what was essentially a buffer zone between the Crow and Sioux lands.

It was doubtful that the Sioux, with the war in the

east against the white armies, would consider antagonizing the Crow on their western boundary.

Justice sat alone, hatless, watching the fire, which was fifty feet away. The shadows concealed him, comforted him. The stars were brilliant beyond the glow of the fire. Diamonds splattered against the black velvet of night. Ruff studied the constellations for a while.

"I thought you might like a last cup of coffee."

Justice glanced up to see Marguerite standing over him, a cup in her hand. Ruff nodded and stretched out a hand, taking the black, hot coffee. Marguerite smoothed her skirts and stood there hesitantly.

"Sit down," Ruff offered. "If you have a minute."

Marguerite did so, and as she sat beside Ruff she saw him put something aside. She knew what it was, and she grimaced with the memory.

Ruff looked at her over his coffee. "Does that bother you still?" he asked.

"That . . ." She looked at the scalp once again. "Yes, it does."

"Well, that's right, I suppose."

"It doesn't bother you?" she asked.

"No. But then, I've been out here a long while. I've become like my enemies, like my friends. It is our way. Bravery is honored here. Ritual is observed. This Lakota"—he turned over the scalp—"will not meet me on the other side."

"You talk as if you believe there's magic in that." She laughed. The laugh, the smile, faded as Ruff lifted serious eyes to hers.

"They are as liable to be right as we are," he answered. "I do not know. I am among the savages and so I live savagely. There is no respect for a man who will not fight, who cannot hunt on the Dakota plains.

Elsewhere, perhaps there is no honor for a man who would kill, would hunt."

"In Baltimore?"

"Maybe. They honor poets, but when there is work to be done they look for the hunters, the warriors. Here honor is kept until one dishonors himself—within the code no one can take it from me."

"Your own hair . . ." Marguerite hesitated. "You wear it so long. Like Bill Cody and Mr. Hickok. Colonel Custer. Isn't it like throwing down the gauntlet to your enemies? I mean, it seems as if you are saying, 'Here rides a warrior. My hair has grown this long among you. Take it if you dare.'"

"Does it seem like that?" Justice smiled.

"Yes! Is that how you want it? Challenging your enemies? Challenging death? Even your horse, Ruff. You ride out here with a silver-mounted saddle when you know many a man would kill you for that alone."

"Yes. One day someone will." His voice grew serious, hard. "But while I live I will not hide from death."

She scooted nearer to him in the night, her breasts rising and falling with some emotion she could not define herself.

"Then which is the real you, Ruff? Plainsman or poet? Romantic or warrior?"

"There's no answer," he said. "A man is the victim of his times, of his circumstances. Perhaps," he said quietly as the firelight faded, "neither is real. Neither my stunted, savage nature nor my pathetic striving toward something beyond man, toward spirit. . . ." His voice faded away into silent thought, and then as if to end such thoughts he pulled Marguerite roughly to him and kissed her deeply, his hand slipping under her skirt, finding its way to the crotch of her bloomers, where his finger sought and found the warm cleft which was damp through the soft fabric.

"Justice . . ." She kissed him passionately, her hands going to his crotch, finding his long erection. She drew back, her eyes bright. "Let's go off a little ways," she asked.

Ruff got to his feet and drew her to him. Together they walked into the tall grass, the stars twinkling brilliantly overhead.

It was dark and cold as they lay against the earth, and it was Justice's savage nature which controlled him on this evening.

Marguerite lay in quiet, thrilled astonishment as Justice hovered over her, his silhouette against the stars briefly before he got to his knees and began undressing her.

His rough hands tore at her pantaloons, and not bothering to remove them completely he raised her skirt, unbuttoning his pants with one hand.

Then he pressed against her, his fingers preparing her for his cock. He kissed her roughly, and Marguerite gasped for breath as she felt him enter her without preliminaries, felt him drive against her, felt his callused hand on her buttocks, lifting her higher as he slammed it home time and again, his mouth against hers, his breath coming raggedly.

He made love savagely on this evening, and there was something wild and wonderful in his urgency. Marguerite found her own body responding in kind—urgently, demandingly, and she felt a sudden climax well up and burst as Justice, driving deeply into her, using her, came to a trembling, frenzied climax.

Justice lay silently on top of her, the scent of the grass, the woman, and the night mingling in his nostrils. Without speaking he rolled aside, and Marguerite lay beside him, her head on his arm.

She sensed that he did not want her to stay, and so she simply rolled to him, kissing him once gently as her fingers touched his cheek. Then, tugging up her pantaloons, she returned to the wagon, leaving Justice on his back, watching the silvery night.

He had needed her, wanted her. But loving Marguerite on this evening had not been enough to exorcise the demons which rode him, and Ruff knew he would not sleep that night.

He lay quietly against the cold earth, watching as the constellations swam slowly past. A low-winging owl cut a darting silhouette against the sky, and the rising moon glossed the dew-heavy grass of the plains.

Ruff sat up and wiped back his hair. The Denton campfire had gone out, the night was still. And then he saw it, perhaps five miles back—and he stood, eyes narrowing.

A campfire. Like a fallen red star against the dark of the plains, it showed plainly. Someone was back there, still following. The same man? The night rider Justice had seen before?

Why? Who could it be, and what did he want? If he was friendly, why didn't he join them, and if he was an enemy, why hadn't he made his move?

No, this man, whoever he was, whatever he wanted, was simply following them. But why? They could lead him nowhere but into difficulty.

Maybe it was not the same man, but Ruff had a feeling it was. The man who had spoken to the Dentons that night back along the river.

Who? The answer did not come, and Justice stood there silently, watching the fire a time longer until it too went out and the moon was the only light across the Dakota plains.

5

THE LAND BEGAN to rise, the plains giving way to rolling foothills and granite ridges. Here and there now they saw small stands of cedar and of spruce. They found elk in a long green valley and surprised a silver-tip grizzly at his feeding.

The Rockies, aloof, snow-streaked, majestic, seemed to hover over them, though in truth they were still seventy miles distant.

The weather had a hard edge to it now, and Justice kept his big buffalo coat on, occasionally breaking out his heavy badger-skin gloves. There was an icy crust on the rain barrel these mornings, and a hard frost on the grass which glittered in the sunlight in the mornings before the hooves of their horses had marked deep-green circles across the silver of the frost, before the wagon had sketched ribbons of color across it.

Breath steamed up out of the horses' nostrils as they pulled the long grade, moving deeper into the foothills where they crossed an occasional icy rill or wound through a boggy high meadow.

Hugh Denton's temper was short. He was beginning only now to believe Ruff's warnings. They would be incredibly lucky to cross those mountains before the snows set in. If they could not cross now there would be no crossing until spring.

The horses were doing as well as could be expected, but still they were wearing down. The buckskin had broken a leg, and Ruff had had to shoot it. The supplies were low now—Amos had spilled a bag of flour and dampness had ruined the sugar.

Justice had still been wary of game-shooting, never knowing who was roaming those hills, and so the meat was low too. The last of the ham—a strapping bone—had fallen to Dooley's appetite.

They sat atop a low knoll, overlooking a long valley where wildflowers—heartleaf arnica, purple lungwort, and yarrow—still bloomed. A pretty little waterfall ran over the nearly white granite to the south.

"Thank God," Hugh sighed. "A little downhill run for a while."

"No. Let's take that south fork," Ruff said.

"*That* trail!" Hugh frowned deeply. It was barely wide enough for a wagon and ran along a cliff some fifty feet high and upward into the scattered timber beyond.

"It's the best way," Ruff advised him, explaining nothing else. Then he turned the Appy and started walking the long trail, the wind hard off the mountains against him. When he glanced back, the wagon was following.

Justice sat the crest, letting the Appaloosa blow, watching the plateau which rose and then crumbled off, reaching for the high mountains beyond. This was a land of sheer escarpments, truncated valleys, quiet hidden meadows and deep woods. Justice knew it well, and he loved it.

Denton stepped from his wagon, setting the brake with a deep curse. Walking to where Justice sat his pony, he advised the scout, "There's someone out there, watching us. I've seen shadows moving among the rocks, and once a flash of light like a mirror."

"It's all right," Justice told him. Hugh Denton ground his teeth together.

"All right?"

"Yes. They're friends. I've known for quite a while that they were out there." Justice turned in his saddle slightly and looked down at Hugh Denton. "It's kind of a comfort to know you've got friends out there watching over a man, don't you think?"

If that rang a bell with Denton, he didn't let on. Maybe, Ruff thought, I'm wrong. Maybe that lone rider isn't tied in with the Dentons. Or it could just be that Denton was a good poker player.

"Let's get on down," Ruff said.

Amos had pulled up, and he looked at the fading sun, which glittered on the distant peaks, slowly sinking into a notch in the mountains, leaving the valleys in shadow.

"What about camp?" he asked. "I've got a hunger in me."

"Don't worry, Mr. Denton," Justice said. "We shall eat tonight—that I guarantee you. Tonight we shall have all we want to eat and then some."

"I saw an Indian!" Marguerite said excitedly, lifting a finger to a jumble of boulders back among the cedars.

"It's all right," Ruff assured her. "They're Crow. Friends of mine. Just a man counting heads so's they can plan for dinner."

"Friends?" Denton laughed. "I've heard no Indian is a white man's friend."

"Nothing could be farther from the truth," Ruff said seriously. "Many men have lived among various tribes, sharing their food, their wars, their women . . .

the white man was almost always accepted as one of their own. Until recently. You'll not find a fiercer enemy than an Indian, Denton—but I'll be damned if I think you could find a better friend.

"And the Crow—they're my friends. They'd share their last meat with me, and have." Ruff glanced toward the red setting sun and smiled at Marguerite, who still looked nervous. "Let's get on down—they're expecting us now."

The Crow camp was set on a grassy bench, screened off by a heavy stand of blue spruce. Smoke curled from their tents into the evening sky, where a touch of red coloring still clung to the clouds. A bonfire burned in the center of the camp, and as Justice led his party toward the encampment a tall brave wearing full ceremonial dress stepped from a tipi and stood, arms crossed, watching.

A dozen dogs started yapping, and that brought the kids running to see what was up. From across the camp, a tall Crow warrior, his forehead daubed with vermilion, strode to where Justice was dismounting and took Ruff's hand warmly.

"You still ride the Nez Perçe horse," the brave said, patting Commodore's shoulder.

"I'll ride him until he can run no more," Ruff answered. "He is a bond between us, Fire Sky."

"And Dooley Dog!" The Crow laughed as the little white dog circled him excitedly, his mouth opening in soundless barks. "He still has not learned to speak."

"Where I ride a silent dog is an ally, a speaking dog a liability."

"It is so," Fire Sky agreed. He put a hand on Ruff's shoulder. Looking up, the Crow warrior saw Marguerite sitting on the wagon seat and asked seriously, "Is this your woman, Justice?"

"I am scouting for them, Fire Sky. These people are

looking for their father's body. It is in Camas Meadows."

"Across the mountains!" Fire Sky shook his head. "It is too late to travel the high passes, Justice. But not too late to meet Shoshoni."

"I know it—these people do not understand all of that, though. They are from far away."

"We will have to speak of this later," Fire Sky said. "For now—come with me. I will have Commodore taken care of. Look," the Crow said, nodding toward the large tipi, "Elk Tooth has dressed for you. We will smoke, eat, talk."

The warrior put a hand around Justice's shoulder, and together they walked to where the old man stood. Elk Tooth was no longer well, apparently. Beneath the seamed leather of his face an unhealthy yellow showed. But he took Ruff's hand warmly, his old eyes sparkling.

"He-who-fights-our-enemies," Elk Tooth said with evident pleasure. "Come into my tent. Bring your friends. We will eat, talk."

"I am ashamed to enter your house without offering gifts," Ruff said. He was breaking etiquette, he knew, but Elk Tooth shook his head solemnly.

"You have given before—many times. Do not bring gifts like a stranger; enter my house like a son."

The tipi of Elk Tooth was warm and large, as befit a chief of the Crow. Hudson Bay blankets were spread on the floor, and a small fire burned in the center of the tent.

The Dentons had followed Ruff into the tent, and they sat well back and to one side as Elk Tooth filled a clay pipe with a mixture of willow bark and tobacco, puffing contentedly on it as the aromatic smoke rose from the bowl.

He passed the pipe to Ruff, who took three puffs

and handed it back. Elk Tooth must have noticed that Justice did not offer it in turn to the Denton brothers, but he never so much as lifted an eyebrow. The old chief read the small omission clearly—these men who rode with Justice were not his brothers, but only men he traveled with.

"Fire Sky says you must go through the high mountains," Elk Tooth said.

"Yes," Ruff answered. "It is for these people. Their father was killed by the Shoshoni. His body must be returned to his home ground."

Elk Tooth understood that motive. "This man . . ." He looked at Marguerite. "He was a warrior?"

"A blue soldier," Ruff told him.

"Then it is doubly important," the chief believed. "What you are doing is right," he said to Marguerite. "But are you not afraid to go among the spirits who certainly dwell on that battleground?"

"No," Marguerite answered with a smile, "not so long as Justice is with us. He fears nothing."

There was a hint of facetiousness in Marguerite's words, but if Elk Tooth read it in her tone, he gave no indication.

Seriously he answered, "I know Justice better than you could. I know he does not fear the Shoshoni or the Sioux. But I know Justice respects the spirits of the dead. Am I not right, Justice?"

"You are right," Ruff said soberly.

"Yes." Elk Tooth nodded, putting the pipe aside as two of his wives entered the tent with bowls of pemmican and maize, squash and venison steaks. "But why have you stopped here, Justice?" the old man asked. "Only to honor me?"

"I have come to visit my old friends," Ruff agreed. He took a bowl from one of the squaws and tasted the food before continuing, "But also to ask for help.

For supplies, and for some of your young men to travel with us."

"We don't need no—" Denton interrupted, but he shut up as Justice's cool eyes met his.

"But we do, Denton," Ruff responded. "Those mountain trails are like nothing you've ever seen. Chances are we won't make it alone."

"Winter is close upon us," Fire Sky put in.

"I know that," Justice replied. Now was the time the men must be hunting meat to feed them through the long winter. "That is why I suggested young braves—those who have no family yet might be willing to travel a little way with us."

Elk Tooth was silent, as was Fire Sky. Justice knew what they were thinking. Firstly, the young warriors, even those with no family to provide for, could hunt and help the tribe as a whole. Secondly, to travel the Shoshoni side of the mountains was to invite trouble.

"We will council on it, Justice," Elk Tooth said finally. That was all the answer Ruff could hope for, and he nodded. Elk Tooth was the leader of the Crow, but even as war chief he could not simply order men to travel with Ruff. Justice knew and understood that.

The night was cold. Outside, clouds blew past before a strong wind. The Crow camp was silent now except for the occasional cry of a baby, the bark of a camp dog.

"Hugh doesn't like this idea of yours," Marguerite said. She had slipped up beside Ruff in the darkness, and now, holding a shawl around her, she watched the tall man, trying to guess his thoughts.

"He will—later. He doesn't know what those mountains can be like."

"Will there be fighting—on the other side?" Marguerite asked.

"Very likely," Ruff told her frankly. "We were un-believeably lucky with the Sioux. I can't expect such luck to continue."

Slowly Ruff walked her back toward the wagon. "These people seem to set store by you," Marguerite commented. "They treated that horse of yours like a sacred animal."

"I've been one of them, that's all." Ruff shrugged. "We've fought side by side, shared campfires." They stood now in the shadow of the wagon, the pale moon shining through the deep, dark ranks of pine. "As for Commodore—why, he's a war prize, you know. The Nez Perce breed Appaloosas. Each spring when the snows melt the Nez Perce come through the mountains and out onto the plains, hunting, raiding like all these tribes do.

"Well, I happened to be here one year when they hit the Crow camp. I killed a man and captured his horse—that's all. That's where old Commodore came from, and the Crow remember."

"Then I can't understand why you would ride that horse onto the western slopes," Marguerite said, waving a hand. "Isn't that where the Nez Perce live?"

"Yes. Likely they'll be north, maybe holed up for winter."

"But it's a risk! A useless risk! They'd spot one of their own horses a mile away, wouldn't they?"

"Likely," Ruff had to agree. "But Commodore is my horse. I'll ride him."

"He's a trophy! A token of your bravery, like an-other scalp," Marguerite said with exasperation.

"Exactly."

"Maybe you are crazy. Did you ever think of that, Mr. Justice? Hugh thinks you are, and he's got me leaning in that direction. What you are doing . . . it makes no sense. None at all!"

"Not to you." Ruff smiled. He looked back toward the Crow camp. "But these people understand it very well. They wouldn't think much of me if I was afraid to ride that horse."

"Then maybe you do belong among them," Marguerite said, slowly shaking her head. "Because I don't understand, not at all. Perhaps you are only a savage. Only a lost, bloody savage."

Then she was gone, clambering into the wagon, and Justice was left alone in the night. He could hear the constant slapping of the rocker's runners against the wagon bed, and he turned, walking through the cedars at the camp perimeter. It was cold out, but Justice liked it on this night. He moved through the trees, the moonlight illuminating his path.

He found a huge, water-polished boulder near the small stream, and he sat on it, watching the moon reflect in the water, listening to the night sounds. The wind moved in the trees, rubbing branch against branch. In the cattails frogs grumped. A nighthawk called from a high ridge.

She came from out of the shadows, and the moonlight was on her soft face. She stood off a few feet, just watching Justice, who sat perched on the rock, his hat beside him.

"Hello, Four Dove," he said finally. "Come nearer."

Slowly she walked to him, her hands behind her back, her head slightly down. Her long dark hair was braided on one side. She wore white elkskins, and she smiled faintly as she saw what Justice wore.

"You still wear the shirt I made for you."

"Yes."

"I have a new one for you, Justice. I worked all last winter. It is very beautiful. I made eagles with red beads. . . ."

"You didn't have to do that. You don't have to keep giving to me."

"I could give you no son. A shirt is not much, Justice."

She slid up beside Ruff, and his arm went around Four Dove. It seemed she fit there naturally. It seemed as if they had been sitting in this same spot only yesterday.

She turned those big, doe eyes to him and said teasingly, "Now you bring women with you . . . are the plains so lonely?"

"I've only been traveling with her," Ruff answered. "Anyway—that does nothing for the loneliness."

For a while they sat there quietly, neither saying a word, watching the dark water, the rippled reflection of moonlight, the trees which swayed slowly in the wind.

"Then you have no new wife?" Four Dove asked.

There was a smile on her lips, but her eyes were damp. Ruff drew her nearer.

"No new wife," he said without looking at her. She tilted her head against his shoulder, and Justice put a hand on her dark, sleek hair. "Is everything well with you, Four Dove? Where do you stay?"

"Everything is well. I still live with my sister and Wildcat."

"He's a good man."

"Tonight they are not at home," Four Dove said, lifting her eyes, which were brighter now, expectant.

"No?"

"They have gone to the cliffs to pray. To pray for a miracle, Justice. To pray I might still bear you a child."

"Four Dove, we . . ."

"I know." She rested her hand on his sleeve. "But it

is something Wildcat and Sister Sweet Water wished to do. When they saw you ride in . . ."

Ruff shook his head, watching the moon dim behind the black-and-silver clouds. It was something he thought done with, something he tried not to think of anymore. But he glanced at Four Dove, and he found those faithful eyes on him.

"It can hurt nothing," Four Dove said. She stood, taking his hand, tugging him gently to his feet. "The tent is there. It can do no harm but only make you feel good, maybe chase away some loneliness. Come, Justice. Let Four Dove be your wife again one night."

Together they walked through the night and found Wildcat's tipi, which was set a little apart from the main camp, close up against the seventy-five-foot lodgepole pines.

Inside embers burned, lighting the tent with a dull, warm glow. There was a clean, new bed made.

"It has been a long trail, Justice. Let me do your bath," Four Dove suggested. By the dim light Justice watched as Four Dove untied her dress and let it fall to the floor of the tipi. She stood there unashamed before her former husband, her girlish figure glossed by the firelight. Ruff pulled his shirt off over his head, and Four Dove sat at his feet, pulling off his boots. Already Ruff was feeling his blood rise, and as he stepped out of his trousers, Four Dove studied his half-erect cock, a tender smile on her lips.

"Come now," she urged him. Naked, Justice squatted near the glowing embers, and Four Dove unfolded a heavy blanket, which she threw around his shoulders. She poked at the embers a little, stirring them to life.

When the fire glowed more brightly, Four Dove returned with a pot and dipper. She threw water on the stones in the fire then, and the steam rose, filling

Justice's blanket, spiraling upward toward the vent in the tipi's roof.

With the blanket around him and the steam, it wasn't long before Ruff's pores began to open and the sweat trickled down his throat, his legs, as he watched the naked, fluid Four Dove moving around the tent, bringing more water, taking a handful of herbs from a small straw basket.

Some of the leaves—which Ruff thought were dried sumac and crushed lilac—she threw onto the steaming fire, the rest she ground into a bowl which was filled with thick, creamy yarrowroot soap.

Ruff's hair hung damply across his face, and the steam rose so furiously that he thought for a moment that the blanket had caught fire.

Four Dove hummed as she worked and as his eyes swept over her, enjoying the pretty sight of those small, dark-nippled breasts, the lean, smooth thighs. Justice recalled vividly a day when he had wandered in from a blizzard and Four Dove had been there to comfort him the same as she now was.

That day the snows had come in rapidly and Ruff had walked twelve miles through subzero temperatures, staggering into camp, certain that he had frostbitten toes. Yet she had been there. . . .

"Enough, Justice," Four Dove said. And Ruff got up, gratefully throwing the blanket aside. He lay on his stomach on a buffalo hide, and he closed his eyes, feeling Four Dove's nimble fingers rub the soft soap between his toes, into his calves and thighs. Then she straddled him, kneading his buttocks and lower back, her hands tracing circles of sheer luxury against his flesh. Ruff opened an eye, and looked once at the low glow of the embers, seeing a strand of Four Dove's hair as she hummed and worked on his shoulders, turning around so that she knelt in front of Ruff now, and he could feel her thigh graze his cheek.

"Over now," she ordered, and he did so. She soaped his chest and stomach, and it was enough to put him to sleep, there in that warm tipi, the cold night locked away from them. But he could also catch Four Dove's sweet scent, see the curve of her beautiful ass, the lazy pendulous motion of her breasts, and that was enough to keep him awake.

Now Four Dove worked on his thighs and crotch, her fingers light, deft, as she worked her soap in, spending an extra moment with his shaft. Ruff closed his eyes, letting the sensation, the warmth, rush over him.

"Up again," Four Dove said, and Ruff nodded, standing. He crouched near the embers once again and Four Dove took her water pot, ladling it over his shoulders, his back, rinsing him clean.

Then once again he was obliged to crouch in the steaming blanket, and this time Four Dove added more of the aromatic herbs.

Finally he was through, feeling squeaky clean, new. Standing, he let Four Dove work her way around him, rubbing him dry with a towel. When she was through, satisfied with her work, Justice sat in the chair.

"You still keep the chair," Ruff said with a smile. Four Dove nodded. She sat beside him, her hands and chin on his knee, her eyes bright.

"You made this chair. And so it has remained with me. No one sits in it."

It was a simple piece of furniture Ruff had devised with four crossing pieces of wood and a leather seat and back. He sat silently in it now, watching as the embers died to a golden glow, as Four Dove sat at his knee.

"All these things . . . your memories, Four Dove. You must not keep them, cling to them."

"Sh!" Four Dove put a finger to her lips. "Not tonight, Justice. Do not tell me sad things tonight."

Her arm curled around his thigh, and her fingers gently took his cock. She looked at it lovingly, holding it in her palm while the other hand toyed with the head of it, causing it to twitch and yearn for more.

Four Dove cupped his balls in her hand and leaned her head against his thigh, gently caressing them. She placed his cock against her cheek and sat utterly still for a long moment, and to Justice it all seemed some sort of ritual.

Ritual or not, her hands and the sight of her sleek body in the dull glow of the embers had inflamed him. Yet he did not move except to stroke her soft hair. She did not move, and he heard her whisper—a whisper not meant for his ears.

She began then to work more passionately on his erection, watching as it throbbed and grew still more swollen. Four Dove's eyes were fixed upon it, and only now and then did she glance up at Ruff's eyes as her fingers worked magic against him.

Now there was a trembling growing in Justice's thighs, and Four Dove knew he could not hold back much longer. Slowly then she rose and untied the braid in her hair.

Taking Ruff's hand, she drew him to his feet, and as he watched, his eyes drinking in the soft curves of Four Dove's body, her silky flesh, she turned and leaned against the chair, her head low so that her profuse dark hair fell across it. She spread her legs and lifted onto tiptoes, reaching back between her legs to find Justice, who had eased up behind her, his hands sweeping over her lovely, smooth ass.

Four Dove's hand found his cock, and looking between her legs she guided Ruff in, her breathing erratic, her legs trembling.

Her fingers held his shaft, and Ruff eased forward, sinking into her warm, fluid depths. Four Dove still watched, her eyes glittering as he penetrated to the hilt, and she reached back again, holding his sack against her.

Ruff moved in slow circles, smearing her against him, her buttocks against his thighs, her body quivering as he moved. Then gradually he began stroking, watching as he slid in and out of her, watching her smooth back, those voluptuous hips, his hand searching her.

Now he began to move more rapidly, plunging deep, and Four Dove responded by swaying against him. Her hands gripped the chair tightly, and her head hung limply as he drove against her, his body urging him to fill her, and he felt himself peak, felt his onrushing climax. He worked against her more feverishly now, his blood racing in his veins. And then he reached it, and he pressed against her, holding her roughly as the orgasm drained him.

He leaned far forward, his chest against her back, fondling her pendant breasts, kissing her shoulders. Four Dove reached back between her legs and held him in, not letting him move, wanting every last moment.

The embers had died and the camp was silent. The buffalo robes were warm, and the woman sleeping beside Ruff was breathing quietly, deep in a peaceful dream.

Through the vent in the tipi's roof Justice could see a single blue star—stark, glittering against the cold sky. He watched it until it drifted out of sight, and then he too slept, the woman cradled in his arms, and the dream did not come.

6

Morning broke clear, a brilliant rosy dawn painting the eastern skies, shadowing the broken hills of the Crow homeland.

Four Dove was not in the tipi when Ruff got up, and so he dressed, walking out into the busy camp where women were already preparing buffalo hides, smoking meat, carrying water while the clamor of kids racing their dogs through the clearing resounded through the camp.

Hugh Denton, wearing a week's growth of whiskers and a sour expression, was hitching his horses as Ruff walked up. Ruff nodded to the man, got a grunt in response, and walked on around to the back of the wagon, noticing Amos, who was sitting off at some distance under a tree, whittling.

The wagon was empty, and so Justice waited. After a time he saw Marguerite leading Candida back toward the wagon. The girl was unsteady, as she had a right to be—that sitting for day after day was just no good.

Marguerite smiled as she approached, but it was an odd little smile. A little tight, Justice thought. From the other side of the wagon Fire Sky was arriving, and he stopped short, studying the two white women.

"A ghost girl," Fire Sky said in a low voice.

"A what?"

"You know, Justice, a girl who travels with ghosts. Like the Mountain Woman in the old legend. This one"—he nodded at Candida—"she travels with ghosts."

Fire Sky was deadly serious, and it was easy to see what he meant. Candida, wearing her white chemise, her mass of dark hair curling across her shoulders and breasts, was a beautiful thing. But her skin was chalk-white from not being in the sun, her eyes empty of all light.

Marguerite helped her sister into the wagon. Fire Sky, still standing beside Ruff, watched as she was seated in her chair and began that absent, methodical rocking.

"This is no good," Fire Sky whispered. Marguerite flipped the canvas flap shut and together Fire Sky and Justice walked off a way.

"I would believe it," the Crow said, "if you told me you were going into the mountains to search for that woman's soul."

They could still hear the rocking of that chair, and Ruff's mouth tightened a little. He shook his head without replying.

"Elk Tooth has spoken to the young men," Fire Sky told Ruff. "Some will go with you. Three men."

"I'm grateful," Justice said sincerely. "Are they men I know?"

"I think so. The wild one—Cada—he will go anywhere for excitement."

"He thrives on danger. But he is a good man."

"And Three Fish."

"That's a surprise," Justice commented. Three Fish was a taciturn young warrior, an enigma even to the

Crow people. He was given to long, solitary journeys, returning without explanation at odd moments. Justice knew of the man, but they had never even spoken. The single time Ruff had tried, Three Fish had simply gotten to his feet and walked away. But the man was a wonder with horses and with a long gun, and that was what counted.

"You said there would be three men traveling with me, Fire Sky. Who is the other?"

"I. I ride with you, Justice."

"Elk Tooth would allow the future chief of the Crow to ride with me?" Justice asked with the barest of smiles.

"Nothing could stop me," the warrior said seriously. "You are my friend—I have not forgotten the old days. If you ask for my help it will be given without question."

"I appreciate it, Fire Sky. Deeply."

"But if the snows come, Justice," Fire Sky had to tell him, "we must return. We cannot be caught on the western slopes for a winter. You know this."

"I know it." For the Crow to be wintered on the western slopes where the Shoshoni and Nez Perce lived was tantamount to suicide. Not that they lacked the courage to attempt such a winter, but they would be three men lost to the tribe; and the tribe was everything—it must be if they were to survive. "I appreciate whatever you can do . . . and I know it is plenty."

They left that morning—none of them wished to delay. Fire Sky led out, his medicine feathers knotted into his hair, with Ruff following. Then the Denton wagon came, with a sullen Amos riding behind it. Three Fish and Cada followed.

The day was clear, the last clouds having blown away, and the sun was bright upon the land without a shadow to stain the brilliance. Except perhaps for the shadow which Four Dove cast as she stood beside a wind-torn cedar, watching as Justice rode out.

The cold wind blustered up the long canyons, and the way was rugged and narrow. They were in dense forest at times, the day turned nearly dark by the deep ranks of spruce.

They wound up a precarious trail along an out-cropping of granite. Water seeped across the trail, and they had to hitch three extra horses to the wagon to pull the long grade.

Exhausted, they reached the crest, overlooking the meadows below, the far-stretching stands of virgin spruce and cedar. Justice sagged onto a rock, wiping the sweat from his eyes.

Fire Sky sat beside him, and it was the Crow who spoke up, saying what they all knew.

"That wagon, Justice. We cannot take it up the trails we must follow."

"I know it. I'll talk to Hugh."

Hugh Denton was leaning against the front wheel of the wagon, his face red, his breathing labored. His lips tightened when he saw Justice approaching.

"The wagon's got to go," Ruff told him flat out. "We'll never make it towing that thing."

"We need the wagon," Denton objected. "For Candida."

"For Candida? We can tie her onto a horse, rig a travois—something. You're risking her life letting her sit in there. Maybe it was all right on flat ground. But here there's more chance of dumping her out the back, watching her go over the side with that wagon on one of these high trails."

"I won't hear of it," Denton barked. "The wagon stays."

Amos chimed in, "How the hell we gonna carry Pa's body home on horseback?"

"That can be done with a travois too. We'll be riding through Gallatin in a few days. Leave the wagon there. We can pick it up on the way back."

Then Justice turned and walked away. The Dentons watched him go, moving easily, that sheathed Spencer in his hand.

"The hell with him." Hugh Denton spat. He turned to Amos and to Marguerite, who had climbed into the wagon box. "He knows," Hugh said.

"How could he?" Marguerite asked.

"How the hell should I know?" He eyed her coldly. "Maybe certain people talk too much when they're in the throes of ecstasy."

"Don't be stupid, Hugh," she answered sharply.

"What makes you think he knows?" Amos asked. He was still watching Justice from under those thick eyebrows, his jaw set.

"The Indians," Denton said. "In case you haven't noticed it, brother Amos, we no longer outnumber the tall man. He's got three of his savages with him now—you realize what shape that leaves us in, don't you?"

"I heard him say them Crow wouldn't cross the mountains."

"That's what he says. Now, I'm telling you he knows," Hugh Denton insisted. "That's why he wants to ditch the wagon."

"Is it possible?" Marguerite wondered. She watched as Justice spoke for a moment with Fire Sky before once more stepping into the saddle of that Appaloosa, and she decided anything was possible with the plainsman.

"How about the way he plays up to Candida?" Hugh reminded them. "Yes—I think he knows. He's sticking his nose in where it don't belong, and for now . . ." Denton glanced at Cada, who slowly rode his pony past. "For now he's got the upper hand. For now."

Hugh spun away angrily and walked to the saddlehorse, stepping into leather as Three Fish, the silent one, watched with eyes which spoke nothing.

They camped in the pines; there the wind which ruffled the campfires was not so fierce. The weather had been building again, with clouds swelling against the skies, and the higher they rode the colder the wind.

The Dentons kept to themselves, and Justice camped with the Crow, or rather with Cada and Fire Sky. Three Fish, ever a loner, had withdrawn into the hills to sleep alone.

The wind twisted the two eagle feathers Fire Sky wore in his hair. He held out a bit of venison to Dooley, but the dog would not take it. Fire Sky laughed.

"He is a one-man dog, this one. He would not take that meat if he was starving."

"No, I don't believe he would," Ruff answered. Nor would he take any attention from the Indians. Cada stuck out a hand, and Dooley's lip curled back, exposing white teeth and pink gums. Cada's hand withdrew.

"Aye! A fighter." The warrior laughed. "I believe he has counted strong coup as you say."

"Not such strong coup as you, Cada," Justice said, "but he is a fighter."

Dooley trotted to where Justice sat on a skinned, nearly white pine log and went to his belly, resting his head on Ruff's boot as he eyed the two Crow.

"Maybe he does not like Indian smell," Cada suggested, but Justice shook his head. Many a dog had been trained to smell Indian or white. Some folks didn't believe it possible, but a white man sweated sugar, salt, and coffee and his scent was altogether different because of it.

"He's just a loner, Cada—like Three Fish, I guess. Some reason or the other he doesn't like folks other than me much."

"Three Fish likes no man," Cada said. He glanced toward the hills where the third Crow had disappeared. "And no one knows why that is either."

"A ghost rides him," Fire Sky guessed. Cada shrugged, and they let the subject drop, not wanting to speak of a brother behind his back.

Cada had another thought. "I have been thinking, Justice. If it snows or does not, I will go to the western slopes with you."

"Cada is always eager for a fight," Fire Sky said with a shallow smile. "I believe he hopes that we do meet the Shoshoni."

"Yes," Cada answered thoughtfully. "And so . . . ? I am a warrior. I was born only to fight. When I die I will die in battle."

"A man so eager will find that battle soon," Fire Sky told him. Cada only shrugged, and then he rose, stretched, and swaggered off into the woods. "He is still a very young man," Fire Sky said to Justice. "With the ideas of the very young. Elk Tooth does not wish us to fight the Shoshoni. I will speak to him seriously before we reach the high mountains."

"All right," Ruff answered, knowing that Elk Tooth's object was to avoid a battle with the Shoshoni. He smiled at Fire Sky and added, "But if there is trouble *before* the mountains, I am glad to have that warrior with me."

"You expect trouble?" Fire Sky inquired.

"I don't know. There's something going on here that I can't figure—maybe you've felt it too. Did you know that someone is following us?"

"I know," Fire Sky answered. "Three Fish saw someone, and he told me. How many men he could not tell. Perhaps two. But only one, he thought. It occurred to me that it was someone you had an agreement with, Justice."

"No. All I know is that one man met with the Dentons—or one of them—and has been following ever since."

"I do not like that," Fire Sky said. "I like no one on my backtrail."

"Nor do I," Ruff replied. "But he's back there—or they are. We've got to live with it."

"Or die with it," Fire Sky said somberly. There was no answer to be made to that, and so Ruff poured his coffee dregs out into the fire, watching it burn low as he and Fire Sky, out of caution and habit, both withdrew a little way into the woods and rolled out their beds.

They were two days and nights in the tall timber before they rolled down onto the long grasslands once again, with the town of Gallatin still a day ahead.

Beyond Gallatin the road climbed once again. But it was no gradual lift of the land. There the Rockies thrust up against the cold skies. To the south, beyond Yellowstone, they could see the awesome bulk of the Grand Tetons, eternally snow-streaked, raw and aloof.

The wind shrieked across the plains as they rode. The low roof of gray clouds slipped past, and the grass wriggling in the wind gave the impression of a trembling earth.

It was Amos Denton, riding out to the south, who saw them first, and his shouts brought their heads around. Amos came fogging it in, whipping his pony as he came, and behind him the Indians.

Hugh snatched up his rifle and already had it shouldered before Justice could reach the wagon. He called up with authority to Denton: "Don't shoot! Put that thing away."

"Shoshoni!" Denton called back angrily.

"Put it away, they're not Shoshoni!"

They slowed the wagon and then stopped it, the Crow sitting off to one side, Justice to the other as the Indians rode up. A party of twenty men and half that many women, they were Assiniboin Indians heading north for their home along the Canuck border.

Their leader drew up next to Justice, keeping an eye on the Crow. He held a hand up, and Justice responded.

"No fight," Justice said, and the man nodded.

Their horses were loaded with buffalo hides and meat. It had been a successful hunt, apparently. Now the Assiniboin too would hole up for the winter, their larders stocked.

"Have you seen the Shoshoni?" Ruff asked their chief.

"No Shoshoni. Blackfoot two days back." There were two fresh scalps knotted into the mane of the horse this Indian rode, and Justice would have bet there were no longer any Blackfoot back there. "Where do you ride?" the chief asked. "Shoshoni country?"

Justice illustrated with his hand. "Over the mountains."

"Oh no," he said flatly. "Too late for mountains."

Opinion on that seemed pretty unanimous, Justice

had noticed. Why then was he crazy enough to try it? That army pay wasn't that good.

"Better you find Shoshoni than winter up there," the Indian said, nodding toward the Rockies, which were lost in the low, dark clouds. "You cannot fight winter, no?"

The chief looked Justice over once more, not failing to identify the Nez Perce horse. Then he glanced at the Crow. Cada had come forward a hundred feet, his eyes eager. Then the Assiniboin lifted his hand again, and at his signal the hunting party drifted past.

Justice rode back beside the wagon, watching as the hunters and their women streamed northward. Marguerite suddenly stood in the box and pointed.

"My God, Justice! They've got a white woman."

Ruff had seen her already. A woman of twenty or so with dirty red hair. She wore buckskins and rode beside a thick-shouldered warrior. She did not look toward the wagon.

"She was white. Once," Ruff answered.

"You can't let them take her!"

"Didn't you hear me? She's no longer white. Maybe they've had her since she was a child. She's dead to those who know her, those who maybe looked but did not find her."

"You won't lift a hand?" Marguerite asked in astonishment.

"It would do no good," he said. Then slowly he turned Commodore and led off to the west, the Crow following him.

They could no longer see the mountains, nor the color of the sky. The earth seemed paved over with black, drifting clouds. Far off a bolt of lightning crackled brilliantly, and the grass trembled again. The first drops of rain were scattered, large, but within minutes it was raining buckshot and Marguerite was soaked through.

She hardly noticed. She sat watching the small band of Assiniboin until the rain swallowed them up as well.

7

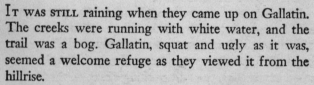

It was still raining when they came up on Gallatin. The creeks were running with white water, and the trail was a bog. Gallatin, squat and ugly as it was, seemed a welcome refuge as they viewed it from the hillrise.

There wasn't much to Gallatin—three pole-and-sod buildings, a falling-down stable, and the trading post which had been built thirty years earlier by a French trader named LaCroix who had been scalped by his first customers.

"It's not much," Justice observed, "but it will get us out of the weather. Could be they've got some coffee."

"They've got a fire going," Marguerite called through the rain. "That's paradise enough for me just now."

It was true. Smoke lifted from the trading post, mingling with the gray of the sky. "Let's get on down," Justice said.

"Not us," Fire Sky answered.

The rain ran across the Crow's shoulders, lacquering his face. Justice glanced at him.

"No? Why not?"

"We do not know who is there. It could mean trouble to take Indians."

"You go where I go," Justice said with steel in his voice.

"No. This is best, Justice. We will make a small camp." He nodded. "There, by the oaks. We will share a buffalo-skin roof. It is better."

"Let the man stay if he wants, Justice!" Denton shouted. "Let's get ourselves down and out of this." As if to punctuate that desire a brilliant chain of lightning sparked against the dark skies and thunder boomed across the grasslands.

Fire Sky was adamant, and maybe he was right; still, it rankled Justice a little. They rolled down off of the wet hills and onto the flat where Gallatin sat huddled. The town was a bog; silver ponds of water stood in the road, the rain pocking them. A tilted sign painted on a weathered plank read, "Gallatin, Mont."

There was smoky light showing through the oilcloth window of the trading post, and Denton, hunched in the box of the wagon, the water streaming off his black slicker, headed his team that way.

A rough pole building stood to one side of the road, and on it was a second sign, obviously done by the same hand. It read, "Gallatin Stabel."

"Let's see the horses are taken care of first," Justice shouted.

"The hell with the horses," Hugh mumbled.

They were going nowhere without horses, but Denton seemed unconcerned by any of it. Justice waited as the Dentons clambered down from the wagon, Marguerite assisting Candida.

They rapped heavily on the rough plank door to the trading post, and Justice heard a cough and a rasping voice and saw a thin blade of light as the door swung open, admitting them. Then Ruff, scowling, unhitched their team.

Ruff turned the team, leading Commodore and Amos's horse. Slogging back through the mud under skies as dark as night, he went to the stable.

McCurdy glanced up from his meal and nudged Tim Simmons. "Looky there," the big man said.

Simmons too looked around, watching as the two pilgrims and two women came through the front door of the trading post, the rain spattering the floor briefly as a gust of chill wind whipped through the room.

Teerlinck was dozing in the corner, but Simmons reached over and slapped his shoulder, waking him. The redheaded man broke off his snoring and yawned, and then his eyes came wide open as he saw the two women.

Pretty they were, both with a figure that made a man look twice. The younger one looked to have something wrong with her, Teerlinck noticed. They had to lead her to a chair and sit her down.

"What the hell you make of that?" Simmons asked in a low voice, scratching at his whiskered chin.

"I don't know," McCurdy answered. Big John McCurdy had led a life of wandering and violence. He and Simmons were both wanted in Kansas and Colorado. Teerlinck had thrown in with them in Missouri, and the three of them had celebrated this new association by knocking over a bank in Joplin and shooting three men.

Together they had stuck up four stages and two more banks, but they had netted little. Those farming-community banks held little more than seed money, and a good spree in Kansas City would eat that money up in a week.

Most of their time was spent lying low, evading the law, and looking out for easy marks. Not the month before the McCurdy gang had terrorized a small community on the Yellowstone, raping and robbing, finishing by burning down a farmhouse and shooting yet another man.

That had netted them nothing as well, and now McCurdy had settled for waiting out winter in Gallatin. But these pilgrims might offer something in the way of opportunity.

McCurdy watched as Sam Trammel, who ran the trading post, wiped his hands on a towel and walked to the plank table where the pilgrims had taken their seats.

He let them order their food, which would be coffee and buffalo stew, since that was all Trammel had, and then, trying to appear amiable, the big man sauntered over.

Hugh Denton glanced up at the unwashed, big-shouldered man who hovered over him, blocking out the light. "Can I help you?" Denton asked.

"That was what I was meaning to ask you," McCurdy answered. He managed what he thought was a friendly smile and then he plopped down on the bench beside Hugh, nodding at Marguerite, who did not respond.

"I'm not sure what you mean, Mr. . . . ."

"McCurdy," he answered, poking out a dirty, thick hand, which Hugh Denton took reluctantly. "What I mean is, sir, it's rare to get strangers in these mountains what with the Indian trouble and all . . . rarer still this time of the year. Most rare with women in the party."

All the time McCurdy was talking he was sizing the Dentons up, trying to assess their worth, to measure the problem they would present if McCurdy decided to cut their throats.

"We are in need of no services," Hugh said. He withdrew his arms from the table as Trammel slapped down a plate of buffalo stew. Trammel spared a glance at McCurdy, wanting no trouble on his property.

McCurdy looked into the corner, where Tim Simmons and Teerlinck, playing with a greasy, dog-eared deck of cards, seemed oblivious to this.

"It's only that this is a rugged land," McCurdy went on. "To those that don't know the country, it can be murderous. May I ask where you are traveling?"

"To the western slopes," Denton replied shortly.

"Very hazardous this time of year," McCurdy persisted. Now where in hell were these pilgrims going on the western slope in dead of winter? he wondered. Pilgrims they were, but they didn't look that stupid. The woman had those dark eyes on him, and McCurdy smiled toothlessly, getting no response. That rankled him, but he swallowed it. He was growing more curious.

"I know most of those high trails, you see," McCurdy continued, "Mr. . . . I'm sorry, I never did get your name."

Hugh Denton sighed heavily, and with his mouth full of stew said, "Denton."

"Mr. Denton." He nodded. "You see, me and the boys are a bit down on our luck just now. For a few dollars we'd be happy to guide you through."

"We already have a guide," Denton answered sharply.

McCurdy didn't like any man taking that tone with him—he had killed men for speaking to him like that. But he choked it back and managed another smile.

"Well," McCurdy shrugged, pushing back from the table, "if you change your mind . . ."

The door banged open with a blast of cold wind behind it, and the tall man stepped into the trading post. McCurdy's head came around, and he frowned.

He noticed too that Denton's jaw tightened as the man in buckskins strode to the table, laying his rifle on the bench beside him as he scooted to it, water running from his clothing, his long dark hair.

"Next time you neglect those horses it will be the last time!" Justice said, his voice throttled with anger. "Those horses are the means to survive. You neglect them and you're cutting your own throat."

"I was going to take care of them after I ate and warmed up a bit," Hugh shot back.

McCurdy looked from one man to the other, a smile twisting his rubbery lips. Justice glanced at him, and McCurdy returned his stare coolly.

"Who's this?" Ruff wanted to know.

"Only a friendly stranger," Hugh answered. "For God's sake, Justice, get off my back!"

"I'd be happy to," Ruff answered. "Damned if that wouldn't make me happy . . . but you haven't shown me yet that you can wipe your own nose without help, Hugh."

Then Ruff stood up and walked to the counter, where Trammel placed a pot of coffee before him. McCurdy watched him go.

The big man stood. "That's your scout? Kind of hard-shelled, ain't he?"

"He's a bastard," Hugh snarled.

"Yeah, well . . . me and the boys will be around, Mr. Denton. Just in case something does come up. Like I say, we know these trails."

McCurdy nodded to Marguerite, who sat woodenly watching, then he spun on his heel and walked back to the corner table, pouring himself a drink from the bottle the three men shared.

"What are you thinking, Hugh?" Marguerite asked finally. Hugh Denton sat there, staring into his greasy coffee.

"Just what you think," he answered. Amos Denton burped, and Hugh glanced at him with disgust.

"You don't know anything about this McCurdy."

"I know he's not Justice," Hugh snapped. "I'm telling you, Marge," he said, his voice lowered, "Justice knows something. And with those three Indians he can do whatever he wants. We've no longer got anything to say about what happens."

"You really think . . ." Marguerite could see Ruff's straight, broad back as he hunched over the counter, speaking to Trammel as he sipped his coffee.

"I say we cut him loose," Amos said, leaning back in his chair. He wiped his mouth on his coat sleeve and stretched. "Cut him loose before we reach Camas."

"McCurdy . . ." Marguerite objected, but Hugh silenced her with a gesture.

"Men like that can be handled. Look at the oaf." Denton glanced at McCurdy and his men, contempt obvious on his face. "I'd rather deal with ten like that than one like Justice. And those Indians—I don't like riding with those Crow either. What do we know of their motives? No—I'd take a chance on a man like McCurdy anytime."

Marguerite suddenly appeared forlorn. She sagged in her chair. "I'm beginning to be sorry we ever started this."

"You won't be sorry when it's over," Hugh said. He reached across the table and patted her hand. "I promise you that."

He looked at Candida, who was immobile, rigid.

"Why don't you see if there's a room where you can clean her up a little?"

"All right." Marguerite had regained her composure. She pushed her half-eaten dinner aside and got up, the scraping of her chair bringing Ruff's head around. She smiled at him, a smile which faded as soon as his back was turned.

"Do what you think is right, Hugh," she said. "I've trusted you this far."

She stuck out her hands to Candida, who took them and rose automatically, following along as Marguerite went to where Trammel was stacking tinned goods. The storekeeper pointed to a side door, and they heard Marguerite mutter a thanks.

Hugh lingered over his coffee, listening to the rain sweep down. After a time Justice left, carrying two boxes of cartridges, and Hugh nodded to Amos.

Together they walked to the corner table, where Tim Simmons had just picked up the pot with three fives. McCurdy glanced up as he dealt.

"Yes, Mr. Denton?"

"I've decided," Hugh said, glancing nervously toward the door. McCurdy noticed the motion, but said nothing.

"Decided what?" he asked. He slapped the deck aside and folded those massive forearms on the table before him. There was a nasty, oily gleam in his watery brown eyes, and for a moment Hugh hesitated.

Taking courage, Hugh told him, "Decided I would like you to scout for us. You and your men." He glanced at Simmons, who spat on the floor, wiping his beard with the back of his hand.

"Certainly." McCurdy nodded. He looked quickly at his partners. Teerlinck kept his head down, studying the hand he had been dealt. "What kind of pay did you have in mind?"

"Two dollars a day. Apiece. Plus provisions, of course," he added hurriedly.

"Well . . ." McCurdy leaned back, rubbing his jaw. "That sounds fair enough, Mr. Denton. But there's a problem, ain't there?"

Hugh blinked and shook his head uncertainly, "I don't . . ."

"Your old scout, Mr. Denton. Who's going to fire him?" McCurdy asked with a slowly spreading smirk.

"Why, that's no problem," Denton said without conviction. He hadn't thought things out that far. It wouldn't be easy to get rid of Justice if he didn't want to pull out. But then, why wouldn't he? He himself had expressed dissatisfaction, an unwillingness to go up into the mountains.

"Don't worry," McCurdy said, and his smile was gone now, replaced by an ugly cold expression. "I'll see that your Mr. Justice is dismissed good and proper. Once John McCurdy has spoken to a man they generally come to an understanding."

"I don't want . . ." Hugh began, but McCurdy came to his feet, his bulk blotting out the lanternlight. He stepped nearer to Hugh Denton, his tobacco and leather smell filling Hugh's nostrils.

"Don't worry, Denton. I know what you want—you want the man fired. Well," he said, "let me handle it. When McCurdy fires a man, he stays fired."

He had an ugly little smile on his face, and as Hugh watched with satisfaction and trepidation, the big man buttoned his buffalo coat. Then McCurdy pulled on his hat. Checking the loads in his pistol, he shoved it into his coat pocket. Then he turned, and Denton saw the man stride to the door, going out into the rain and wind.

"You don't have to worry," Tim Simmons said. He spat again, spreading jacks and threes on the table. "You'll only have yourself one scout when McCurdy gets back."

Teerlinck collected the cards and shuffled them. As the Dentons moved away, he looked up to Simmons.

"I don't get it," he said. "What the hell's McCurdy up to? We don't have to go through all this play-acting to follow them down the road and cut their throats."

The bearded man poured a drink and downed it. "Didn't you hear their name?" Simmons asked.

"Denton?" Teerlinck shrugged. "I heard it—is it supposed to mean something?"

"It means a whole lot more than two dollars a day." Simmons winked. "Don't you worry, partner. Old John knows what he's up to." He nodded at the deck of cards. "Deal 'em again; I'm feelin' suddenly lucky."

8

The stable was cold and dark. Rain racketed off the flimsy pole roof, and the wind blasted through the chinks in the walls. Trammel had told him there no longer was a stablehand in Gallatin, and so Ruff pitched the hay into the bins himself, adding a scoop of oats to Commodore's feed.

Then, working by the feeble light of the lantern which he had hung on an upright pole, he curried Commodore, rubbing him down and covering him with an old horse blanket he had found stashed in the corner.

Then he set to work on the Dentons' horses, after first hanging the harness, taking the time to repair a torn strap. There wasn't much oil in the lantern, and now it burned low, fizzling as it would for a time before it burned dry and went out.

By the last light Ruff spread his bedroll in a empty stall which he had shoveled out. The stable was musty, smelling of horses and manure, but it was dry, or nearly so, and he had slept in worse places in his life.

The horses were better company than many men he had traveled with, discounting the smell . . . and come to think of it, there had been a few men who smelled a deal worse.

The lantern flickered out, and Justice took off his hat, hanging it on a peg. He unbuckled his gunbelt, but kept it close at hand. Stretching out, he shifted until he found a nearly comfortable position, and then, hands behind his head, he closed his eyes, listening to the incessant rain.

The door banged open and the cold wind washed in. Ruff was to his feet in a moment, but it was not quickly enough. The big man hovered over him, and in the darkness Justice heard the distinctive, chilling sound of a hammer being drawn back.

Justice had had no reason to expect trouble, and he had reacted too slowly. His gun and his bowie were both out of reach. The big man stood there in the darkness, holding the big blue Colt in his meaty hand.

"Just stay right there," McCurdy growled. But Ruff was having none of that. Stay there and die!

He lunged out of the darkness like an uncoiling cougar, and this time it was McCurdy who was too slow, too complacent.

McCurdy knew he had the upper hand, and he had been quietly gloating. His intentions had been to demand that Justice pull out, and if threats failed, to batter the plainsman, shoot him if necessary. But while McCurdy had been planning what he would do, Justice acted.

He came up like a shot and drove his body into McCurdy's, his shoulder catching the big man in the chest. The Colt erupted with thunder and flame over Ruff's shoulder as he barreled into the big man.

Justice drove McCurdy back against the wall of the stall, and they slammed into it, McCurdy's air whooshing from him. A plank cracked, and McCurdy's grip on the pistol he held was broken.

A horse sidestepped and whinnied. A second answered it, and Justice drove a fist into McCurdy's face. But McCurdy was bull-tough and bear-mad. McCurdy wasn't much, but if there was one thing he was, it was a fighter. He had brawled his way up and down the Mississippi and across bloody Kansas.

Justice's right hand jerked the big man's head back and split the cheekbone, but McCurdy was far from through.

McCurdy drove a knee up, and it glanced painfully off Justice's thigh. At the same time the big man's hands went to Ruff's face, and he dug with his thumbs, trying to gouge the eyes.

Ruff twisted his head frantically and threw two hard rights to McCurdy's ribs. They were softened by the bulk of McCurdy's buffalo coat, but he still felt them. The wind went out of him, and he came up with a roar as Justice got to his feet and stepped back.

McCurdy held his hands low, like a wrestler, as he moved in, only a hulking shadow against the darkness of the stable. Ruff shot out a straight left which missed, a second which caught the big man on the temple, slowing him a bit.

But only a bit. McCurdy was relentless, and he was intent on his work. His size and strength had won many a fight for him. His style, if it could be called that, was simply to drape himself over his opponent and slam away with those piledriver fists.

Ruff had seen this kind of fighting before, and he didn't mean to let it happen. He jabbed at McCurdy's head, snapping his head back, bringing a gush of hot blood from his nostrils.

McCurdy lunged forward clumsily, and Ruff sidestepped him easily, slamming his fist down on the back of McCurdy's neck. McCurdy fell to the stable floor, but he rolled and was up in a second.

It was then that the faint light caught the silver of a tool, and McCurdy snatched it up. He held the shovel high and came in, slicing with the shovel blade like some great battle ax, and Ruff backed away, ducking the shovel, which would have sliced his head off.

McCurdy, grinning, flayed left and right with the shovel, the implement making menacing whooshes as it cut the air close to Ruff's head, his shoulder.

Still Justice was able to evade it, backing constantly away, his hands out to parry when possible. And then he felt the wall behind him and knew he was in trouble.

Moving in confidently, McCurdy brought the shovel down with an ax stroke, and it rang against the wall as Ruff ducked, then drove forward under the shovel, battering McCurdy's face with two hard rights which set the bells ringing in McCurdy's head.

McCurdy staggered back, Ruff's pounding fists following him, driving into his ribs, then hooking over his guard, slamming into his face. McCurdy threw up a hand in defense, felt it slapped aside, and another granite-hard hook jarred his head.

McCurdy stepped back farther and tripped over his own feet as Ruff's relentless fists rained blows on him, and he was driven down, landing hard on his back.

"I'll kill you, you bastard," McCurdy growled, but he was in no shape for killing flies. He got to his knees, started to rise, and watched helplessly as Justice met him with a driving right which snapped back his head and drove him to the stable floor again, his head cracking against the hard-packed earth.

Justice hovered over him for a minute, blood trickling from his own mouth, his clenched fists dangling at his side. Then he walked to where he had left his gunbelt and leaned over.

That brought a stab of pain to his ribs. The big

man had gotten in a few good punches. Ruff strapped his pistol on and wiped back his hair, leaning momentarily against the stable partition, taking in several deep breaths. Then he planted his hat and walked back to where McCurdy, groggy on hands and knees, waited, shaking his buffalo head.

"Get up and get out before I kill you," Justice said coldly.

McCurdy nodded heavily. He had to take hold of the pole upright to get to his feet, and when he was standing he stood eyeing Justice, his face puffy, his eyes dull.

"I didn't think you were that much man," McCurdy said, his voice slurred.

Ruff didn't respond. He nodded toward the door.

"Get out and stay out."

The stable door opened slowly, the wind seeping in, and for a moment Ruff paid no attention, but now he was aware of the shadows filling the doorway, and he glanced that way, his hand slowly dropping to the butt of his holstered Colt.

"I wouldn't do that," Tim Simmons said. The two men stepped into the stable. They carried a lantern, and by the light Justice recognized them from the trading post.

"You can let that gun drop," Simmons said, and Justice did so. Teerlinck had stepped in behind Ruff, and in his hands was a ten-gauge express gun. There was no arguing with that sort of rough logic.

McCurdy had been standing there stupidly, a dazed expression on his thick, bruised features. Now that expression changed into vindictive anger, and he stepped near to Justice, practically breathing in his face.

"You know what I'm going to do to you now, pretty boy? It'll be slow, I promise you. Maybe I'll slice away some of the gadgets the ladies like first—"

That expression which had gone suddenly hostile changed abruptly once more. McCurdy backed off a step, his eyes going beyond Justice to the door of the stable.

Teerlinck had been the first to notice. A sharp jab from a lance head had caused him to drop his scatter-gun and lift those hands for the ceiling.

The Crow stood there, eyes black and savage. Fire Sky held his Winchester at waist level, the hammer eared back, his finger on the trigger.

"Kill them here?" Cada asked with what seemed a little eagerness.

"No." Ruff picked up his Colt and dusted it off. "Take their guns . . . throw them out," he said with weariness.

"What was it they wanted, Ruff?" Fire Sky wanted to know. "Are they old enemies of yours?"

Now that was something Ruff didn't even know. Puzzlement furrowed his brow as he looked from Simmons to Teerlinck and finally back to McCurdy, realizing that with all the blustering and hollering McCurdy had never actually said why he was after Justice.

"Well?" he asked the big man.

"I don't like you," McCurdy muttered. Silently he was cursing Hugh Denton for not having mentioned the Indians who were obviously traveling with them.

"That's not good enough," Ruff said. Now he was angry. Fed up with this. The trail had been hard enough without being jumped by every thug and cut-throat along the way.

Ruff stepped toward McCurdy, but a voice inter-rupted his motion. "I'm responsible, Justice."

Justice looked to the doorway, where the Denton brothers stood. Angrily Justice started that way, but Hugh held up a hand.

"I've asked this man to guide us through to the western slopes, knowing you don't like me or the mission much. He said he would let you know that you were fired. . . . I didn't realize how roughly he would inform you. Perhaps Mr. McCurdy misunderstood."

"I don't think he misunderstands now," Ruff answered.

McCurdy wasn't bad at thinking on his feet. He added, "I thought this man was a-threatenin' you and your sisters, Mr. Denton. If I done wrong, I apologize."

McCurdy turned soulful eyes to Ruff. Justice was buying that explanation like a three-legged horse, and when McCurdy stuck out a hand, Ruff ignored it.

"You invited these men along?" Justice asked, turning back to Denton.

"Yes. So you see, Mr. Justice, there's no need for you and your Indians to continue on."

"No? I think there is."

"What possible . . ."

"It's my assignment, that's what," Justice replied shortly. "And I'll be damned if I'll turn my back on duty."

"But I'm releasing you from your duty," Hugh said, his hands spread.

"I guess only Colonel MacEnroe can do that, Denton. He's not here."

"Well then, by God, we'll all have to get along." Denton lowered a trembling finger. "Because McCurdy and his men are riding with me."

"That's your decision, I suppose." Justice shrugged. "But you might as well stick a gun to your head."

"I know you don't like this," Hugh shot back, "and I know why. I know why you've got these Indians with you!"

The man was irrational, his face red, as he leveled

that finger at Justice, then at each of the Crow in turn.

"By God, Justice," he screamed, "you won't beat me at this!"

"Denton," Justice said quietly, "a man like you don't belong out here. Certainly not in those winter mountains. I won't beat you." He shook his head. "You'll beat yourself, man."

Hugh turned and went out into the rain, Amos following. McCurdy had a tight little smile on his puffy lips, and he shouldered past Justice, muttering, "It's a long trail ahead, pretty boy."

"It can be, McCurdy. It can be if you let it. If not . . . you'll find out for yourself that a long trail can end most abruptly."

McCurdy cornered Hugh in the trading post, and he was having trouble controlling his anger as he said, "You never told me he had Injuns with him. That don't leave us with good numbers."

"The Indians will turn back when the snows come—that's what Justice says."

"But will they?" McCurdy asked.

Hugh shrugged. "If they don't—maybe someone could encourage it." Sparing one meaningful glance at McCurdy, Hugh walked to the table, where Marguerite, hands in her lap, waited.

"What happened?"

"We're all going."

"*All* of us?" she glanced at McCurdy and shivered. "Hugh, I don't like this. It's getting too complicated."

"You think so?" Hugh lifted an eyebrow and held Marguerite's hand a moment. "I think it's working out fine. None of them will try anything until we're on the western slopes. Then . . ." He shrugged. "Let them have at each other. It'll be fewer men to worry about."

"Will it? I'm already worried, Hugh. McCurdy—he gives me the shivers. If a man like that ever found out . . ."

"He won't, will he? Like I said, I can handle men like McCurdy. And Justice, well, we won't have Mr. Justice to worry about much longer, I don't think. After all," he said, stretching and yawning, "we don't need him anymore. We've a friend who can take care of the man now."

Marguerite was uncertain. She said nothing else, but her mind hummed with worry. This plan of Hugh's, so logical in Baltimore, had snarled upon itself and become studded with danger for all of them. She glanced at McCurdy again, imagining what a man like that was capable of. It was enough to start her shivering again, and she scooted nearer to the fire, pretending it was only the cold.

The rain had changed to sleet, and it drifted down in a heavy wash, melting to slush against the dark earth. Ruffin Justice stood watching the night for a time, looking toward the trading post where still a dull light burned.

Then he looked westward, into the wind, where the far, hulking mountains were hidden in the mist and clouds. He walked slowly back to the stable, his unsheathed Spencer across his arm.

Inside the doorway he stopped and watched the weather build. There was a scuttling noise behind Justice, and he turned sharply, his hand tensing. He stopped short. The familiar white face looked up at him, stubby tail waggling.

"And where were you when I needed you, Dooley Dog?" Justice asked with a smile. He squatted on his heels and scratched Dooley's ear.

Then he heard a whimpering, and he glanced to the

stall nearest them. A fawn-colored muzzle protruded from under the lowest slat. Justice stuck out a hand and the little bitch crawled to him, going to her back to have her belly scratched.

"Well," Justice said, patting Dooley Dog, "I guess that's a good enough excuse." He smiled then and stood, but as he turned again toward the open door the smile slowly faded.

It was a bad night, with more to come.

He curled up again, this time with his pistol in hand, with Dooley by his side. He was working his way deeper into a fix, and he knew it.

It would snow soon, and hard unless he missed his guess, and that meant Fire Sky and the other Crow would have to return. Meanwhile Denton had hired McCurdy and his crew on . . . and there was the man on the backtrail, whoever he was. Justice had no doubt he was a Denton man.

He had told Denton that it was duty keeping him on this job. Was that sensible? Ruff knew he would be lucky to see the end of this trail, the way feelings were running, the way the weather was running. To be trapped in those high mountains was by far a more terrible death than a gunshot.

No, it wasn't duty—duty be hanged when it was senseless duty, unwanted, unappreciated. There was another reason Justice could not be run off.

And he lay there in the darkness thinking of Candida, of that beautiful, soulless woman of the night.

9

THEY ROLLED OUT in the cold gray of predawn. A
slow, steady drizzle fell from the mottled gray skies.
The green of the grass and the deeper blue-green of
the trees appeared unusually rich in contrast to the
dark grays all around.

The footing was sodden, and the horses moved
warily. Ahead the fantastic bulk of the Rockies
loomed above successive tiers of mountain valleys.
Fourteen-thousand-foot peaks which scraped the belly
of heaven itself, they were a broken, jumbled mass of
sheer slopes and broken, weather-honed ridges.

It was a land of primordial chaos. In times long
past, eons ago, the land had exploded, thrusting up as
pressures within the core of the earth sought release.
Then the mountains had been born.

The pressure of Hades thrust them up, and they
rose steaming into the clear air, lava running from
their cheeks. They had risen, broken, folded, and been
thrust up again. Now they loomed, mocking man's
smallness, standing cool and aloof, scarred by the centuries, some of the jagged edges softened by uncount-
able winters. Grand, majestic, defiant.

Yet men like these would scoff at their grandeur—Justice turned in his saddle and watched as the Denton wagon rolled along, as the sullen McCurdy crew trailed it, their collars turned up to the cold and damp.

It was a broad, joyous land up there, at the right time, under the proper circumstances. Justice and Four Dove had hunted there one spring, the skies blue, far-reaching. The mighty stands of timber stretching to the skies, the barren, snow-streaked pinnacles above the timberline. There grizzlies roamed, and cougars, moving like a tawny streak of lightning.

Justice had known this stretch of mountains well—here he and Four Dove had fished for trout in the high country streams—icy, quick-running fountains. There were deep canyons flooded with fern and hanging gardens. Badger lived among the timber, and elk.

They had made love in the sweet-smelling summer grass. All eons ago.

But this was winter, and the world had turned over too many times. The mountains thrust up cold heads against gray, hanging skies and the wind blew like the cold breath of hell down the long slopes, roaring up the canyons as the timber shivered along the frozen flanks of the peaks.

And Four Dove was not here.

They climbed higher, the horses trampling down mushrooms of all hues—purple, pale yellow, iron gray—products of the recent rains.

Now the valley began to narrow and funnel into the deep spruce beyond. They would be in the timber for two days at least, and then the trail twisted upward toward the Hump, as it was called, easing past the timberline and onto the cold gray flanks of the mountain. That was where they would be tested.

They no longer stopped for a noon meal. The wind was cold, and it was better to be moving. The hours in the saddle, or perched on the wagon seat in the damp and chill, knotted their muscles, brought a stiffness to the joints, and seemed to strangle off circulation.

They camped the second night in a teacup-sized valley where grass for the horses still grew—and Justice was worried about that as well. How would the horses be fed on the high trail? While the others sat around the fires—the Crow apart from the others—Justice cut what grass he could. It was rough, clumsy work with only his bowie to utilize, but it might at least save Commodore's strength.

He packed it back to the wagon, stowing it in an unused corner without asking the Dentons' permission.

"High-handed, ain't he?" McCurdy asked, loud enough for Justice to hear.

"Crazy." Amos laughed. "That little bit of grass ain't gonna do any good." Amos had changed. With the arrival of the McCurdy gang, he had become more assertive, swaggering as he moved, bold as he spoke.

The clouds had parted long enough for a crimson shaft of sunset fire to flood the peaks around them and tint the meadow to a suffused purple as Justice made his last trip.

"Well now, Candida," he told the silent girl who sat rocking, a heavy shawl around her shoulders, "they think I'm crazy now. I guess they call you that too." Justice sat on the tailgate, mopping his neck and face with his kerchief; the wind was chilling on his work-heated body.

"You should be out there, riding with us," Ruff said, smiling at the girl, looking into those black eyes where nothing answered his smile. "It's a glorious sight—these mountains. Great purple ranges broken by peaceful valleys. The wild flowers are gone now, but there's a stark beauty to the land. There's snow on the high peaks, and Lord, the spruce and cedar, all wet with the rain—why, it sparkles when it chances to catch a shaft of light. The streams are running full. That white water roars down the canyons, and when it catches a rock at times it sprays into the air, making tiny rainbows. . . .

"I've brought you something I promised," he said.

Reaching inside his shirt, Ruff withdrew a folded piece of paper and told her, "Now don't you laugh at this, Candida—I once shot a man for laughing at the wrong time. But then he was an ugly one . . . you're so pretty, I guess you could get away with it.

"Maybe it's not much, but it's well meant."

And then he read to her, his voice low as the shadows closed around them.

> "In your eyes I saw great beauty,
> Eyes that once were star-caressed
> And love-lit, laughing, vital, blessed.
> On your lips I saw a faded smile—
> Lips which used to laugh, now dressed
> In silent sorrow, loneliness.
> Come out of winter, silent bird,
> Let your summer song be heard,
> And my lips touch your silent lips
> So they may live again."

Ruff glanced up. "Well . . ." He shrugged and folded the paper once more, tucking it back inside his shirt. "At least you didn't laugh."

He stood up and went to her, kissing her head once gently before crouching down.

"You've got to fight this off, Candida." He searched

her face and then stood, touching her soft dark hair again with his lips before stepping to the tailgate and slipping to the ground, tying the flap behind him.

Marguerite was standing there when he turned around. She looked weary. She had her arms crossed against the cold of the evening. Stepping nearer, she looked up to Justice and said, "You never do give up, do you?"

"What do you mean?"

"Her." She nodded toward the wagon. "This business with Candida. She'll never come out of it, you know—the doctors are unanimous."

"Are they? Well, I've seen a lot of things happen no doctor could explain. It costs me nothing to try with Candida."

"Maybe I'm just jealous," Marguerite said. She stepped to him, her body pressed against his, her hand resting on his thigh.

"Really?" Ruff smiled. "I didn't think any of you cared if I came or went—unless it was preferring the latter."

"We need you," Marguerite said, turning her eyes down. "But why did you come? After all that happened . . . that still might."

"Because of her." Ruff looked toward the wagon. "And because of you—I'd hate to see you get hurt or stranded, Marguerite."

"Nothing will happen," she said and laughed.

"No? Maybe you don't understand what a man like McCurdy is capable of."

"I don't think I have to worry about that," Marguerite replied.

"I think you should be worried, Marguerite," Ruff said. "After all, it's not like Hugh and Amos were really your brothers and gave a damn about you. If it comes to a time when they have to make a trade-off of some kind ..."

"Not my brothers?" Marguerite laughed, but her face was washed out, her laugh tremulous.

Ruff, leaning against the wagon wheel, went on, "Maybe you don't realize just how valuable a white woman is out here. You know what would happen if McCurdy ever got hold of you? They'd pass you around first—McCurdy, Teerlinck, and Simmons. Each of them after you until you were worn down, dirty, sick.

"When they were through with you, you'd still be worth something. Likely they'd sell you to the Indians—trade you off for some ponies, maybe. The Indians, they'd have their fun with you. A lot of men, one after the other. Then, saying you survived it all in pretty good shape, you learn how to scrape buffalo hides ... and you'd learn good." Ruff lifted an eyebrow. "Because that's what your life would be from then on out. Scraping buffalo hides until you were old and crippled from it."

Marguerite's face was stiff with anger at Ruff, and with horror—for she half-believed Justice. She remembered with stark clarity the redheaded girl the Assiniboin had captured—the total surrender on that girl's face. "It wouldn't happen. Hugh wouldn't allow it."

"Supposing Hugh couldn't stop it? You think he's a match for McCurdy? I don't."

"But ..."

"And it doesn't have to happen that way. Suppose the Shoshoni hit us, as it's likely they will?"

"You're trying to scare me."

"You're damned right. Look, Marguerite. You and I could ride back to Gallatin—with Candida and the Crow. You could wait there for Hugh and Amos to return."

"Them come back—!" She laughed, then shut up, realizing she had said too much again.

"Why wouldn't they?"

"You know. I thought Hugh was wrong, but you *do* know, don't you, Justice?"

"No." He spoke in a low voice, peering at her from out of the darkness. "I don't know your secrets—I'm just trying to help you and Candida. But McCurdy . . ." He looked toward the low-burning campfire. "You can bet he knows, Marguerite. You can just bet he knows—a man like that doesn't do anything unless it's for profit."

"You're trying to trick me!" she said more loudly than she had intended, but Ruff only shook his head.

"No, Marguerite, I'm not. I'm just telling you how it is. It's your decision to make, but make it quickly. After the snows start falling, it will be too late to change your mind."

She looked at him steadily, the wind running icy fingers through her hair. She knew he was telling her the truth, yet she shook her head. "I can't. Maybe it's that I've never learned to trust people. Maybe, I . . ."

She turned then and walked away, putting her shawl over her head as she went to the fire, where the men sat watching her approach.

She poured a cup of coffee from the gallon pot with a trembling hand, and Hugh said, "What's the matter—Justice working on you again?"

"Sort of." She managed a weak smile and then sipped her coffee.

McCurdy was poking at the fire with a stick, and he looked up at her, his eyes glittering. "You see—you ought not talk to the man, missie. Justice, now I hear he has a way with the ladies. He don't fool me none, though."

"What he said made a deal of sense," Marguerite answered softly.

"He's tryin' to spook you, that's all," McCurdy answered.

"Maybe we ought to spook him a little," Simmons said. He had brought a jug of sour mash with him from Gallatin, and his courage was rising.

"You've already tried that," Marguerite said with disdain. Then she turned and walked swiftly away, Simmons scowling after her.

"I'll be turning in too," Hugh said. He stood and nodded at McCurdy, drawing no response. Amos followed his brother, carrying two blankets.

"This'd be a night for it," Teerlinck said, leaning across the fire, his face wolfish in the flickering light. "Cut their damned throats. The Crow would run. I know Injuns. I'd like to lift that woman's skirts . . . God, I would."

"You damned idiot. Settle down and lay off the bottle," Tim Simmons said.

"Don't bark at me," Teerlinck warned the bearded man.

"Tim's right," McCurdy said. "There's profit in this, Teerlinck—if we play it out. And them Crow—damned if I believe they'd run."

Teerlinck hefted his jug, paused, and put it down, corking it. "You say there's gold in this? What exactly is this, McCurdy? I've a right to know what I'm riding these mountains for." He glanced toward Marguerite's wagon. "What I'm passing that stuff up for."

"Sure—you're right." The fire burned low, and McCurdy turned his collar up against the bitter wind. "You've a right to know."

He scooted nearer to Teerlinck, his voice lowering to a gravelly whisper. "It's the Sacramento Express, Bob."

Teerlinck only blinked, and McCurdy put a hand on his shoulder, going on.

"You see, with all that Sioux trouble back on the plains there wasn't no army payroll comin' through. You ever try to get a soldier who ain't gettin' paid to fight?

"Along comes this idea—instead of comin' west, they bring that payroll from California, from Sacramento, you see, then up over the mountains and from there to Fort Ellis, Fort Henry, and Fort Smith—the three garrisons that are cut off.

"The boys along the trail called it the Sacramento Express. Hell, every outlaw worth his salt dreamed of that payroll, and the word had gotten out."

"Yeah?" Teerlinck lifted a dubious eyebrow. "Then how come nobody did hit it?"

"You got to be kidding!" Tim Simmons laughed. "Forty cavalry soldiers!"

"Besides, nobody knew just where they was going to cross the mountains. They had a crafty man ridin' herd on the planning, and he kept it quiet. This man," McCurdy said and winked, "was named Major Seth Denton."

"You don't mean it?"

"I do."

"You mean that gold didn't get through?" Teerlinck's head swiveled toward the dark mountain range behind him.

"It didn't. And not a man made it. The Shoshoni hit them."

Teerlinck's face fell. "Then the Indians got the gold."

"No. That's not what the boys figure down the trail." McCurdy here meant the outlaw trail. News traveled up and down it from one remote hideout to another, and the Sacramento Express had been a main topic of discussion for a long while. "The reason is this. First off, most Indians don't value gold like that. There's many who don't know what to do with it, except make trinkets and such.

"Those who do know—why, they spend it, partner, like you or I would. And ain't none of that new-mint gold showed up yet at any trading post or whiskey runner's stand. No, sir, it's there—somewhere—and these folks know where."

Morning was briefly clear, fading before the shadows of new clouds. By late afternoon the clouds hovered over them like dark dogs waiting to be unleashed. The rain began near dusk, and they traveled steadily upward, seeing the barren gray flanks of the cold mountains through the mist.

The timber began to thin, the footing to grow rocky, with grass sparse. Twice Justice suggested they make camp while they still could find graze for their horses; twice he was ignored.

The mood of the Dentons had shifted. Before he had been a thorn in their side, but a necessary one. Now they trusted entirely to McCurdy. When they spared a glance at Justice, riding that leggy Appaloosa, it was the kind of glance an unwelcome following dog gets.

"Let us go back," Fire Sky suggested as the two men rode side by side. "I can see how it is with these people—they do not want us, do not want your help."

"I can't turn back," Ruff said. "You do what you must."

"I must ride as long as you will have me," Fire Sky said. "Yet," he added, "I have been more welcome among the Sioux."

Justice was appreciative. He realized fully what sort of shape he would be in without the Crow. McCurdy had already shown that he had no qualms about bashing Ruff's head in, if that was what it took. And soon the Crow would have to turn back—the weather would demand it.

Looking to the darkening skies, Justice watched the light, wind-shuffled rain fall, watched the pines swaying before the stiff breeze. Ahead lay the country of never-melting snow. High barren passes where there were no provisions for man or beast. Death traps they were, those high passes. The snow drifted to forty feet or more up there, and once it started there was no escape.

He rode silently on, watching Dooley Dog trot ahead a way, wait, and then begin trotting again.

What was it these folks were after? There was no doubt remaining in Ruff's mind that it was not the body of Major Denton. He knew such motives would not sway a man like McCurdy; nor would two dollars a day. A man would be a fool to ride these mountains for a hundred dollars a day. . . . Ruff smiled, recalling what he was being paid for just that.

No, it was for profit. . . . Then suddenly it came to him.

The Sacramento Express! It had to be. Then Major Denton had been connected with that project, that failed project which had half the soldiers in Dakota Territory grumbling. And somehow the Dentons knew where that gold was, or believed they did. Was it really Camas Meadows or only somewhere nearby?

No wonder they had been jittery, wondering what Justice knew. That Sacramento Express was no secret except as far as the actual route used went. And a man like McCurdy would have heard about it in all likelihood. That explained his presence.

The wind was cold in Ruff's face as he mulled it all

over. It fit; he was sure that was the explanation. Yet it was hardly reassuring.

It meant only that Justice must die.

He looked ahead, catching a glimpse of Candida behind the canvas of the wagon. Dooley ran out ahead once more, and McCurdy was picking his way through a rocky stretch.

The rain had begun to turn to light snow, and the clouds bunched overhead. Far-off thunder echoed up the long canyons. Justice turned up the collar on his buffalo coat, riding with his Spencer unsheathed across the saddle bows.

10

$$\cdots\!\!-\!\!-\!\!\blacklozenge\!\!-\!\!-\!\!\cdots$$

A LIGHT SNOW drifted through the twilight skies. The flakes swirled about in the air and then settled, hissing into the campfire, as Justice sat watching his coffee boil, his mustache and shoulders frosted white.

"This," Fire Sky said surveying the clouds, "it will not last long, Justice."

Ruff glanced at the thin clouds, the patch of clear sky beyond. He nodded his agreement.

"No, not this time."

"More storm behind this one," Cada commented, and again Justice could only nod in agreement.

Fire Sky leaned near to Justice, again trying to persuade him, "Winter with us, Justice. Like the old days. No mountains, no Shoshoni. Only friends and a good woman. . . . Four Dove would like it much."

"No."

Ruff's reply was brief, but he couldn't help thinking about it, as he had thought about Four Dove since leaving the camp. It could be a warm, pleasant winter . . . why would a man choose to risk death?

But he knew, even as that thought flared up—Candida. That helpless, black-eyed woman. Why did they need her? How long would they need her?

He knew one thing—when they were through with

Candida she would be dumped in the snow, left alone. That he could not allow to happen.

Justice poured his coffee and warmed his hands on the cup. "I can't tell you how much I would like to, Fire Sky. To count coup with the Crow, to winter-hunt with friends. But it can't be. Not this year."

"If there will be a fight," Cada said, eagerly leaning forward, "why do we not fight them here, now? Then, Justice, we could return."

"Those who lived," Ruff said, lifting an eyebrow at the overeager young brave. Fire Sky smiled, stretching his arms.

"Who has seen Three Fish?" Fire Sky asked. Justice shook his head. He had not seen the solitary one since breakfast.

"There will be no meat left for him," the Crow said, looking around, hoping to catch a glimpse of Three Fish.

"He's probably seeing to his horse. I'll find him," Ruff said. He started to rise, but Fire Sky waved a hand.

"Drink your coffee. I will see."

Fire Sky stood as Justice squatted down on his heels again, and at that moment the shot echoed down the hillside. Fire Sky turned his head, and Justice saw the front of the Crow's shirt jump and sudden crimson smear across the buckskin.

Fire Sky opened his mouth and sagged to the earth as a second shot scattered their fire. Ruff rolled behind a fallen log, dragging Fire Sky with him, as a third shot and a fourth from a rifle on the hill tore chunks of wood from the log.

Then it was still. Smoke rose from high on the hill, the echoes died away. Fire Sky lay on the cold earth, his chest ripped open by a rifle bullet.

Cada had snatched up his rifle, and now he stood. "I will get him."

"No, Cada!" Justice shouted. "He's got position!"

But Cada could not be stopped. He made a dash for the woods, running in a crouch. Justice muttered a curse and hurriedly cut open Fire Sky's shirt.

"Very bad," Fire Sky murmured.

It was a jagged, ugly wound. Bleeding profusely, it frothed, showing that a lung had been penetrated. "Not so bad," Justice answered. He folded his kerchief and held it against Fire Sky's chest. "I've seen plenty worse."

"On a living man?" Fire Sky tried to laugh, but his voice broke off into a gurgling, strangled cough.

"You'll make it," Justice said softly. "We'll hunt again."

"One day," Fire Sky said. His dark eyes searched Justice's face, and then he closed them. "One day, Justice, we will hunt again."

Then he lay back, life draining from him. Justice could do nothing, nothing. A slow anger began to rise in him, a deep, seething anger. Fire Sky would die—it hardly seemed possible. But death always seems impossible until the moment it happens.

Justice's hand was smeared with Fire Sky's blood; he could feel the Crow's heart beating under his palm. And then he could feel it no longer.

The snow dusted Fire Sky's face, clinging to his hair, his eyebrows. Ruff stayed there, kneeling beside the Crow, for a long minute. Then he heard footsteps pounding behind him, and he spun, drawing his Colt as McCurdy rushed toward him.

"Hold it!" McCurdy called. He slid down beside Ruff. "It wasn't us—not this time. Dead?"

"He is," Justice answered.

"Where's the others?"

"Up there." He lifted his chin. "After the rifleman."

McCurdy nodded, looking again at the dead Crow, at Justice, who still held his Colt in his hand. "I'll get up there and help them," McCurdy said.

"The hell you will," Justice said harshly. He drew back the hammer on his pistol. "Just leave 'em be."

McCurdy's eyes were afire with temper, and his grip tightened on the rifle he held.

"Just leave 'em be, McCurdy—I won't have you running up Cada's back."

"You think I'd . . . ?"

"I know damn well you would," Ruff told him, and his eyes were flint-hard. McCurdy slowly got up, his eyes going briefly to the hillrise. Then, scowling deeply, he rose and returned to the Denton campfire.

The shadows grew deeper, and still Ruff held his position, not wanting to move. Fire Sky was dead— why? The answer was simple.

The bullet had been meant for Justice—he had no doubt about that. He had started to rise to look for Three Fish, and just as abruptly Fire Sky had stood in front of him. Then the rifle had exploded; then Fire Sky had died.

Ruff looked down again at the fallen warrior, fallen friend, and his hand rested on Fire Sky's cool head. Then, shaking it off, Justice stood, filtering through the shadows carefully.

Cada, always the hothead, had made a mistake. Charging up that slope at a man with a rifle who could see him coming was bold, but not clever. Yet perhaps he would manage it. . . .Then the rifle boomed again and Justice cringed.

He stood in the near darkness, listening to the echo die away.

Cada.

The rifleman had killed Cada as well. There was no

doubt in Ruff's mind. It was the same gun—a heavy
Sharps, not a musket-rifle such as Cada carried.

Two Crow dead. And they had come to their death
on Ruff's account. The snows drifted across the gray-
ing skies. It could clear briefly, and then it would
settle in. Winter would begin.

Fire Sky's body was slowly being covered by the
flakes. A day . . . he had come within a day of sur-
viving. With the snows he would have turned back to
his family, his home.

And Three Fish? Justice lifted his eyes to the darkening, cold timber. There was a reason he had not
come in for his evening meal—a quite obvious reason.

Three men dead on his account. Good men. The
sniper had taken them down, as he would attempt to
take Ruff down at the first opportunity. And that
sniper was a Denton man. It was obvious, and Justice
thought he understood it.

He sat now at the base of a massive pine, watching
the world grow dark, feeling the wind in his hair.
Dooley Dog was beside him, his cold nose against
Ruff's hand as the snow drifted past.

It was the Dentons' doing. This sniper—whoever he
was—had been hired to do Ruff in. But not while they
needed him. They were pilgrims in these mountains,
and needed a guide. Well, now they had a new
scout—McCurdy—and that meant Ruff was dis-
pensable.

He would have to be alert every moment from here
on out. The man was up there, somewhere.

Ruff's cold blue eyes lifted to the mountains, now
shrouded in shadow, veiled by the snow. He was
there, and he would kill at the first opportunity, without warning.

Without the Crow, McCurdy would waste no time
confronting Justice either. He had the upper hand,

and he knew it. Did the Dentons know who they were tangling with when they hired the big man on? Ruff doubted it.

They had simply wanted to get rid of him, fearing he knew about their plans, the gold.

McCurdy wanted Ruff dead now, as did the Dentons, probably. The thing was, how long would it be before McCurdy decided to turn on Hugh and Amos as well? It was a tangled web, with all the spiders carrying guns. . . . Ruff patted Dooley's head.

"Stay loose, dog. They've got us in the stew pot and somebody'll be looking around for a match."

Dooley cocked his head, and Ruff smiled at the dog.

Night was closing in across the land; Fire Sky lay motionless beside the dead campfire; the snow fell in a steady wash.

At midnight it was briefly clear, the stars brilliant against a black velvet sky, but to the north the thunder sounded, and by morning the second wave of clouds had settled in, and the snows, which had been thin, light, now became steady and cold.

The temperature had dropped at least twenty degrees overnight as the storm rolled in, and morning brought a strange, icy wonderland.

Justice moved slowly to the campfire. There was ice beneath the new snow, and the trees were hung with balls of ice, like glittering cold Christmas trees. There was little visibility, and the snow was already eighteen inches deep.

Ruff took a cup of coffee from Marguerite, and as he did he noticed her eyes. The tales he had told her came back vividly as winter began in the Rockies—tales of entire herds of buffalo frozen in a gap in the mountains where they had taken shelter from the winds; of cannibalism, and men whose limbs had to be amputated after attempting winter passage.

"How long will it snow?" she asked him, and he shook his head.

"No more than six months."

There was no smile on Justice's lips as he said that. He sipped the coffee, the steam rising into the cold air to be throttled by the icy blast of wind.

"We'd better get it moving and keep it moving," he told Hugh Denton, who walked past, shivering, his breath steaming into the cold, white skies.

Denton only nodded, not arguing as he did reflexively with every suggestion Justice made. The snow was a great convincer, and Ruff could read it in their faces—they were worried now.

And they hadn't seen anything. Nothing yet. Up there—his eyes lifted to the high peaks—the wind could pick a wagon and team up and toss it into the canyons like a leaf. A man without shelter could be frozen to death in minutes. People had smothered in the huge drifts, slowly starved, crushed and buried by sudden avalanches.

"If we're going to get through," Justice told Marguerite, "we'd best get it rolling and keep it rolling . . . because we don't have long, believe me."

The weather was heavy as they rolled out. Justice took the lead, and no one objected. He had to pick his way almost by feel through the narrow gorge and up along the wind-washed mountain slope, the snow swirling all around as the bitter winds rose to a whistling roar.

The wagon, tilted on the slope, kept losing traction on the back wheels, and it skidded uncontrollably away time and again as Hugh Denton fought the team.

Commodore liked none of this; the footing was bad

now—slush over bare rock as they climbed toward the Hump high above. It was bad, and would get worse. Justice was concerned. It was like traveling through a white tunnel. Trees loomed up starkly, suddenly before them. Once they nearly spilled the wagon over a sheer precipice—a whitewater river roared past some three thousand feet below.

Yet Justice kept them moving. To stop, without food, shelter, was to die. If riding was an agony, to rest was sure death.

The land rose more steeply now, and Ruff began to worry that he had lost the trail—he had been over the Hump only once, four years ago on his first visit to Idaho, and then it had been early spring.

He zigzagged up and down the slope, the going hampered by huge jumbles of gray, snow-streaked boulders and deadfalls—long-dead trees, their barked trunks stretched out across the trail like mammoth bones.

Now the trail was lined with aspen, their slender trunks curved by the weight of winter snows. They waved frantic arms against the wind which rumbled through the grove and tore at the canvas of the wagon.

Snow drifted before the wind, obscuring the road so that Justice had continually to search for it, but find it he did, and they rolled on through the blue-white day, through the wind tunnel, fighting off cold and discomfort by sheer willpower.

McCurdy's face was blue with the cold, the fur on his collar thousands of tiny ice needles. Ruff's own mustache was frozen stiff; his body was numb so that it seemed his ears and nose would need only a tap to break off.

Marguerite had given up sitting on the wagon seat, and she now huddled in the bed of the wagon, blankets across her shoulders, as Hugh, his eyelashes frozen, his hands like stone, tried desperately to handle the unwieldy wagon.

They moved briefly through a stand of spruce where the wind was somewhat quieted, the snow shielded from them, and then they emerged again. Below them frozen hell spread out toward eternity.

Gray mountains, visible through the parting snow, merged, thrust up, and fell apart again in chaotic patterns. Their flanks glistened with icy rivulets, and the bottomlands raced with swollen rivers.

"We have to cross that?" Amos Denton, reined up beside Justice, asked in awe.

"I only wish," Ruff replied without glancing at the man.

The road they had to travel was infinitely more rugged, treacherous, deadly.

"We still have to go up," he told Amos. Denton's eyes lifted slowly to the barren slopes, the wind-flagged trees, the deep crevices above, and he silently cursed.

They had three hours of traveling before dark, and they made less than a mile fighting the tedious upgrades, the sudden sharp declivities. Fallen trees had to be cleared from the trail three times, and all had to be done with the icy wind clawing at their faces, snatching at their clothing while the sheets of snow washed down.

At nightfall, exhausted, they huddled together on the lee side of the Denton wagon, the red fire flickering in the darkness, melting a hollow in the snow, which had drifted to three feet even here, under the sheltering outcropping of gray granite.

With the dawn they were rolling, eager to be moving, each carrying a fear of being snowbound in his heart. Justice had taken pity on Dooley, who was traveling with great difficulty, bounding through the snow, frequently sinking over his head. He carried the little dog across Commodore's withers throughout the morning and in the afternoon transferred him to the Denton wagon, where he lay miserably.

They inched their way forward, the wagon tilted crazily at times, at others stuck so deeply that they had to halt and dig it out with their hands, McCurdy grumbling and cursing the entire time.

"How will we ever get back?" an exhausted Marguerite panted to Hugh Denton.

"We won't be coming back. Once we're into Idaho we'll turn south and west. San Francisco will be the next seaport you see, Marge, not Baltimore."

That lightened her spirits a little, knowing now that they only had to reach the pinnacle, the Hump, which could not be far away—a day at the most, Justice had told her. Then it would be down, away from these terrible mountains, away from winter.

She stood against the lead horse, her knees wobbly, to mid-calf in snow, warmed now by the thought of the gold, of the gay San Francisco nightlife . . . and then she looked up and saw him, and Marguerite screamed.

"What?" Hugh spun around, and he fumbled beneath his coat for his handgun.

"There—" Marguerite pointed, but he was gone.

He had come out of the snow, wearing a blue army jacket, carrying a rifle. An Indian with a savage scowl, and a black stripe painted down the center of his rugged face.

"Stay here." Denton rushed forward, then slowed with caution. They were on barren slope, with only here and there a cluster of spruce and a lonesome wind-torn bristlecone pine.

He saw the horse, and his gun came up, but it was no Indian.

"He's gone," Justice told him.

"Was he . . . ?"

"Shoshoni," Ruff said.

"God," Marguerite moaned. The snow was in her tangled hair, her eyes were horrified. "I thought you said they'd be holed up for the winter!" she shrieked hysterically.

"I said if we were lucky they would be," Ruff answered quietly. "Now it could be this is a lone hunter, or it could be he's a castout or a late-comer."

"He could also be a scout for the main body of warriors," McCurdy put in.

"It could be," Justice answered, leaning low from the saddle, his eyes fixed on McCurdy, "but then I know you didn't come into these mountains figuring on making it out without some kind of fight. We'll just have to keep traveling, hoping this man was a loner, or, if he was a scout, hoping that it's not worth it to them to hit a small party like ours."

"Maybe we can outrun them," Hugh suggested.

"Not if they want us," Justice replied, shaking his head. "But it could be the snow will cover our tracks—through there's not but two or three passes through the mountains.

"All we can do," he advised them, "is to keep it rolling and keep our eyes open. We've maybe got enough guns to keep them off if it comes to a fight."

Marguerite stood looking at Ruff even after McCurdy had ridden ahead and Hugh had returned to the wagon. Then slowly she slogged back through the snow, her back bent, her head down.

They rolled ahead, their eyes now searching the snow beside and behind them, their guns loose in their holsters. Everything Ruff had said he had said only to calm Marguerite.

The Shoshoni were out there; and they would be coming.

The sheer stony walls of the narrow gorge rose overhead now as they eased into the pass. The snow was deep, but still they made good time. Only once did they have to clear away some boulders which had slid off.

The snow eased as dusk fell, and the land had become flattened, the pass wider. Still they labored, for the oxygen was thin, but as they emerged from the gorge Marguerite cried out with happiness and Teerlinck let out a whoop.

They had crested the mountains, they had made the Hump, and below the foothills stretched away into Idaho. The skies mercifully had lightened, and here and there a sunspot cut through the film of clouds, shining brilliantly on the white snowscape.

Denton stepped down from the wagon, mopping his brow before replacing his hat.

"Damn me if we didn't do it," he breathed.

Even McCurdy's perpetual scowl was briefly lifted by the sight. Each hour now would bring lighter winds, warmer temperatures, and each mile would bring them nearer to the gold of Camas Meadows.

"You know where you are?" McCurdy asked.

Hugh Denton nodded slowly, first glancing around to make sure that Justice could not hear them.

"I do—I've a map from here on down."

"Then we don't need the plainsman anymore, do we?" McCurdy asked, and Hugh Denton's face was creased by a slowly spreading smile as he answered.

"Not anymore."

11

"You can get him off guard," Hugh insisted.

"It's not that easy anymore," Marguerite shouted back.

"I thought you had him under control."

"You don't control a man like that," she answered.

"There's got to be a way, and it's got to be you. He's got to go, we all agreed. Even you, Marguerite." Hugh Denton's eyes were dark. Looking beyond him briefly, Marguerite saw the clouds drifting past, stretched and swirled by the wind.

Hugh put a hand on her shoulder. "He's not the kind we could trust. He'd never stand for it—I know his kind. The law would be on our tail in no time. There'll be no peace for any of us as long as Justice lives."

"I know it," Marguerite was silent. "There's a way, I think." She looked toward the twin pines which stood near the bluff to the north of camp. "I'll have him over there in fifteen minutes."

Hugh smiled. He leaned forward and kissed her cool forehead. "You're a prize, Marge, you really are."

Then he turned and walked away, whistling, through the snow. From the back of the wagon Marguerite could see Dooley Dog's head protruding, his pink tongue dangling; she walked away hurriedly, the uncanny feeling that the animal knew something riding her back.

There he was—Justice was crouched beside his saddle, his back to her. Commodore blew, and his head came around. Marguerite took a deep breath and tried to still the drumming of her heart. Slowly she walked to him, the wind cold in her face, the brilliant arrows of crimson sundown bright against the snow.

"What is it?" he asked, rising, and her heart jumped. Those cool blue eyes seemed to hold some foreknowledge of what she was about. Impossible! She frowned.

"I have to talk to you; it's important. About Candida."

"What about her?"

"I think . . . let's not talk here," Marguerite said, glancing toward the wagon where Hugh worked at the harnesses. "Over there." She nodded toward the twin pines.

"All right," Ruff agreed. Was there reluctance in his voice, suspicion? Marguerite's pulse pounded in her temples.

They walked to the pines, which stood at the rim of a sheer precipice; the snow was rose-hued under the light of an incredible, crimson sunset.

"What's this about?" Justice wanted to know. His boots crunched through the snow. The twin pines cut dark silhouettes.

"I'm afraid they want to leave Candida," Marguerite said.

They stood now beneath the pines; Justice's gaze swept down the bluff and off across the distance. Camas Meadows was just beyond the low line of snow-covered hills.

"It figures. Tell me, Marguerite, just who is she?"

"Candida?" Marguerite touched her hair nervously, her eyes turned down. "She is Major Denton's daughter. She took her father's death very hard—obviously. She was in a Baltimore rest home when I first met her . . . I was working there. Somehow Hugh found out about the gold, from a western gambler, I think, and when I mentioned Candida Denton, the name rang a bell.

"Going through Candida's things, I found a packet of letters from her father. The last described the route he intended to take."

"I see." Ruff nodded. "But why bring her all this way?"

"Hugh was afraid that Candida might come around one day and talk. Then later he decided that someone out here might know that Denton had a daughter named Candida, and so we kept her with us."

"It's also a reason for having a wagon, which might seem almighty suspicious heading for the mountains."

"Yes." Marguerite sighed. "Nobody ever accused Hugh of being stupid—he had it all thought out. But now . . ." She turned her eyes up to Ruff. "We just don't need her anymore."

"Don't worry," Justice said, resting his hand briefly on her shoulder. "It won't happen as long as I'm around."

"That won't be long," a voice said, and McCurdy stepped from behind the tree, Denton backing him.

Justice grabbed for his Colt, but it was already too late. He saw McCurdy's pistol explode with flame, and he felt the searing impact of a bullet high on his chest. He staggered back, feeling his Colt slip from his hand. Sunset flashed in his eyes, crimson and gold, and Marguerite, hands to her mouth, backed away as McCurdy's gun came up again.

Then McCurdy nodded, and his face went slack. Suddenly he screamed and snatched at his back. He spun around, and Justice saw the arrow protruding from McCurdy's back, and from across the camp he heard shots and yelling.

He saw Denton fire at the attacking Shoshoni, heard the pop-pop of other guns, saw the world spin around. Ruff tried to fight it off, to find his way through the kaleidoscope of pain and blurred light, to grab his gun, but he could not.

He staggered forward, slid back, and then his feet went out from under him and he tumbled through space as he fell from the bluff, the earth far below, cold and savage, rushing up to meet him.

He struck an outcropping, felt the breath slammed from him, felt the fiery pain in his chest; and then he felt nothing more but the all-encompassing cold as the day went dark and silent.

At the wagon Amos had been the first to see the Shoshoni—a rock slipped from beneath the brave's foot as they tried to slip down the slope into the Denton camp.

Amos had turned his head casually and then come bolt upright as a screaming Shoshoni dove toward him, hatchet in hand. Amos fumbled for his gun, but he was too slow. The brave was already on top of him before Tim Simmons's Winchester barked and the Shoshoni went limp as a rag doll, blood streaming from a crater in the back of his skull.

Throwing the brave aside, Denton went to his knee, working the lever on his rifle three times in rapid succession, spraying the hillside with wild shots as a quartet of Shoshoni rode into the camp, their war whoops filling the air.

Teerlinck stood to meet a warrior, and the man

leaped from his paint pony, slamming into the bearded mountain man. A blade flashed and then Teerlinck's gun exploded into the Indian's face.

From the bluff Amos heard the sound of Hugh's rifle firing, and spinning around, he saw the Shoshoni rushing toward him, and he fired from the hip, his bullet cutting a bloody groove across the Shoshoni's collarbone.

Still the Shoshoni ran toward Amos, his eyes glittering, a knife in his good hand, and Amos swung his rifle like an ax, slamming the butt into the Shoshoni's face. The man went down like a stunned ox.

Simmons was behind a nearly square, snow-dusted boulder, and he was firing as rapidly as possible. Amos saw him hit one Indian in the leg, and the brave staggered off into the underbrush.

A Shoshoni dropped from his horse at a dead run and leaped to the tailgate of the wagon. Amos saw him duck inside and then heard a terrible muffled growl, heard a strangled scream, and the Shoshoni flopped from the wagon to the snow, his throat torn open.

Amos shuddered and dashed for the boulders to join Simmons. A warrior rode through the heart of the camp, leaped the campfire, and continued on, hugging the side of his horse as Simmons winged two wide shots at him, standing to follow with a third which sang off into the distance.

And then it was still.

Suddenly silent, with only the cold wind moving the light snow. Teerlinck lay inert against the snow, his blood staining it to crimson.

Simmons walked warily to him and rolled him over. Teerlinck's unblinking eyes stared up into the cold skies.

A Shoshoni, badly wounded, crawled toward the

shelter of the rocks upslope. Coolly Simmons sighted and fired. The Indian jerked and slumped against the snow.

Hugh was coming on the run now, McCurdy behind him. They slowed as they entered the camp and they stopped, guns dangling.

"He dead?" McCurdy asked, nodding at Teerlinck.

Simmons nodded as he reloaded.

"You got a good sharp knife?" McCurdy asked.

Simmons glanced questioningly at him.

"Sure."

"Then run it through the fire," McCurdy said with a grimace. Then he turned, and Simmons saw the broken shaft of an arrow protruding from the big man's back.

McCurdy's heavy buffalo coat had partially protected him from the arrow, which had obviously been shot from some distance. Still it had glanced off his wing bone, chipping it, and imbedded itself two inches deep in his back muscles.

Simmons got to work, straddling McCurdy as he slit alongside the arrowhead. McCurdy grumbled a curse as Simmons went in a little too deep.

"I thought you said that damned knife was sharp!" There was sweat beading McCurdy's forehead when Simmons was finished, despite the cold.

"That was pretty close, John," Simmons told McCurdy.

McCurdy was buttoning his shirt, moving his arm gingerly. "I'll take close over that any time," he answered, nodding at Teerlinck, who lay dead against the snow.

"What about the plainsman?" Simmons wanted to know.

"No need to worry about him," McCurdy said grimly. "We won't be seein' Mr. Justice again." Then he allowed himself a triumphant grin, and Simmons grinned in return. Hugh Denton joined in with a short, sharp laugh.

Hugh was feeling good about things once again. The Shoshoni had been beaten back, and Justice was dead. Too, McCurdy's gang had been cut down to size by the Indian attack. Now they were two against two. McCurdy wouldn't dare make a move until the gold was located, so there was no need to worry about him just now.

Eventually the big man would make his play, no doubt; but then it would be too late—Hugh would make his play first.

His eyes lifted to the snow-washed peaks—was his man still up there, or had the weather or the Shoshoni gotten him? No matter. Hugh figured he had the upper hand now, and a brief, satisfying image of Justice tumbling over the edge of that precipice, blood streaming from his chest, flared up in Hugh's memory.

Humming softly, he unharnessed the horses as Tim Simmons and McCurdy scooped out a grave in the snow for Teerlinck's body. The snow came down heavily once more, but Hugh Denton felt oddly warm as night settled.

There was pain. First the numbing cold and then the hellfire of searing pain high in his chest. Ruff opened his eyes, seeing nothing but the bitter night. He tried to move his arm and found he could not. Rolling his head was an effort, but he did so, blinking away the snow from his eyes.

He could see nothing. It was a world of inky darkness, bitter cold and pain. With his good hand he gently probed the wound in his chest. Painful, bloody, but Ruff decided that that alone would not kill him.

McCurdy's bullet had taken him high on the chest, passing through under the collarbone without breaking it. That was not a serious wound—under other circumstances. But in the freezing night, his body leaking blood, it could very well be enough to kill him.

Where was he? He could not even tell that. He remembered falling, falling, then the agony of impact. His head ached and his ribs were sore—probably several were broken.

The wind howled all around him, and he was lost in the vortex of snow, the hard earth beneath him. His arm! It was immobile, and now as the fuzziness cleared away from his mind he fingered it with his free hand. That arm had feeling in it—plenty of it. It seemed fire coursed through his veins.

Ruff felt around, finding that the arm was pinned under a pile of rubble, and slowly he began clearing it away, digging his right arm free with his left.

That simple operation consumed more than an hour, and when he finally had the arm free he hardly had the strength to lift it. He lay back exhausted, weakened by the loss of blood, taking in great gasping breaths of the frozen air.

He tried to sit up, and the motion brought a surging pain. Ruff's head spun around crazily, and he went out again.

When he came around again it was dead still, windless, and the snow had stopped. The temperature had plummeted, and now as he tried to move he found his buckskins had frozen.

His hair and mustache were weirdly frosted, and his limbs were numb—moving them was like moving logs. He realized his plight fully. He could not remain here unprotected, bleeding. To remain was to die, but he could move with only the greatest of difficulty.

He tried again to sit up, and again until he made it, his head reeling with the small effort. Now Ruff could see where he was. A blur of light hung in the western sky—the moon, half-smothered by the clouds—and by that light he saw his predicament.

He had fallen from the bluff, slammed into an out-cropping and landed here. He now sat on a narrow ledge some hundred feet below the rim of the bluff and two hundred feet above the ground below.

The ledge was no more than twenty feet wide and thirty long, tapering rapidly at the ends. Justice saw grimly that he could climb neither up or down. He was trapped, hurt and cold.

Even if there was a way up, he had not the strength to attempt it. And up there the guns would be waiting for him. The Dentons and the hostile Shoshoni. He had no gun, no blankets, no food, and little hope of leaving that ledge alive.

The winds gusted up the canyons, and he saw the moon blink out as the clouds stirred. Inching back, Justice found a notch in the face of the bluff. Three feet deep and perhaps two wide, it was only a cleft where centuries ago a rock had fallen free and rolled off the bluff, leaving this hollow.

He scooted back into it, his teeth chattering with the cold, his hair in frozen strands across his face. He was warm only where the blood trickled across his chest. Staring out, he saw the clouds shift and roll toward him vengefully.

Ruff closed his eyes and wrapped his arms around himself, shivering violently. There was no way out of this, or none that he could find at night, probably none that his condition would tolerate.

But he swore he would find a way. He swore he would survive.

Survive to find those who had done this to him.

And when he did, more blood would flow. This he vowed.

And then it began to snow again, shutting out the world as he huddled in that shallow notch, red-rimmed angry eyes staring out against the darkness.

12

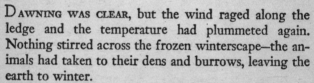

Dawning was clear, but the wind raged along the ledge and the temperature had plummeted again. Nothing stirred across the frozen winterscape—the animals had taken to their dens and burrows, leaving the earth to winter.

Ruff tried desperately to slap the circulation alive. His teeth would not stop chattering, and his skin was blue beneath his buckskins. He examined his chest wound by the clear light and found it jagged, a terrible yellow-and-purple bruise spread across his shoulder, but it seemed to be clotting up and it wasn't that painful, only stiff. Perhaps the cold had numbed it some. His ribs were a different story—two of them, he decided, had broken. They gave him little pain if he held still, but any movement brought a stab of pain which filled his entire side.

There was nothing he could do about that, nothing at all. He certainly couldn't remain still on their account. To remain still was to die, and Justice was not ready to die.

There were some folks out there who had tried to kill him, and a little girl who likely would die if Justice didn't get back to her.

He stood, leaning against the bluff, and the pain

flared up. Gasping, he hobbled forward, looking down the snow-draped bluff to the flat some two hundred feet below. Turning, he looked up.

There was a chute of sorts which a man might be able to climb—a man in good shape. Ruff was not in any kind of shape for a climb out, so it had to be down.

The bluff fell away steeply; it was heavy with snow—and that was his only hope. The snow might slow his descent enough to prevent a fatal fall. It might. It might also ball up into an avalanche, sweeping Ruff down the slope into the gorge with its crushing weight behind him.

But there was no choice, and no time to wait.

Ruff gingerly lowered himself to a sitting position, his legs dangling into space as the cold wind gusted. He spotted a hollow where the snow had collected some forty feet below. If he hit that he might be able to make it—from there on, the incline was less severe. But if he missed it . . . and there was a good chance of that with this wind.

Even if he did hit it, would his battered body be able to stand the impact? If one of those cracked ribs was driven into his lungs, it would put the lantern out permanently.

He waited, the wind blowing his hair wildly, waiting for that wind to subside. And when it did he didn't hesitate, but hurled himself off into space.

He fell for what seemed an eternity, and then abruptly he felt the cold earth come up to slam against him—only belatedly did Ruff consider that there might have been a boulder concealed beneath that snow.

He went feet-first into the drift, his hands out to protect himself, and the breath was driven from him as he was buried in the deep snow.

He had survived, but the impact had driven him deep into the drift, and the snow was even deeper than Justice had suspected. Now there was the very real chance of being smothered.

Desperately he looked up and began clawing his way toward the air, which showed only as a clear, distant spot of blue. With horror he watched as the snow caved in, darkening that patch of light, and he forced himself to calm, to slowly clear away the snow from his face and fight his way up through the drift, packing the snow to form a staircase as he went, moving cautiously now, with the greatest care, to prevent another cave-in.

Finally he was out, and he lay gasping against the cold drift, his heart pounding, shoulder and ribs fiery with pain once more.

With a swimming motion Justice proceeded across the drift, wanting now to be out of there as much as he'd wanted first to be there.

He came to the edge of the drift. There it was piled up against a granite outcropping, and from there it was a drop of another fifteen feet to where the bank sloped away. Ruff leaped again, landing hard, rolling for twenty feet before he could stop his momentum. Then, hair in his eyes, the cold wind blasting against his body, the pain stabbing at his chest, he rose to his feet and walked and slid to the flats below.

Without pausing to rest, Ruff began walking. The snow was to his knees or deeper, and it was exhausting, but he moved southward for an hour. He was hungry and he was cold; he wanted nothing more than a fire, but he kept on, pushing these thoughts aside.

His head rang and spun with weakness. The going was rocky and treacherous. Twice he tumbled into unseen depressions. Yet each time he dragged himself out and plodded on, his eyes fixed on the line of barren, gray oaks to his right.

Finally it struck him, finding its way through his fuzzy consciousness—those trees. The long line of them would seem to indicate a watercourse, and he stumbled that way.

He found the stream, rushing through the trees, ice fringing the banks. He thought it was the Finger Creek, and if it was it ran into Beaverhead, which would take him into Camas Meadows.

Was he right or wrong? Justice shook his head, trying desperately to clear his thoughts. He took a reading by the sun, discovering the creek was flowing west and not south as it should have been, but that meant little; it could be only a bend in the river.

Taking a chance, he plodded on, keeping the stream at hand. The trunks of the oaks were glossed with ice, and from time to time there was a loud crack as an ice-laden branch broke free.

Deliberately Ruff slowed his pace. To start perspiring could be deadly. The sweat could freeze next to the skin, killing a man.

The air was incredibly clear, biting as he sucked it into his tormented lungs, each breath bringing a shot of pain to his ribs.

He crossed a snowy spit and leaped a small feeder stream, the snow crunching as he landed. Then he stopped cold, a chill crawling up his spine. Just ahead, their backs to him, were a trio of Shoshoni.

Justice stood frozen for a brief moment. Then, knowing he had to move, he slipped his bowie knife from his belt sheath and backed slowly away, his eyes alert, his chest tight.

There was a clump of gray, leafless willow behind him at the water's edge. If he could make that . . . then he saw an Indian's head turn, and he stopped again. Perhaps it was only the coloration of his white elkskin clothes against the glaring background of sun-bright snow, but the Shoshoni's head turned back, and Justice in three quick steps was to the willow.

There he waited, crouched on his heels, watching as the Indians shared a meal, cooking over a low fire. He strained to hear their voices, but they were far off, the wind bending their words, and Justice's knowledge of the Shoshoni tongue was not that good.

"Horses . . ." he heard one man say. Then, "Wom-en . . ." and a brave laughed.

Justice crouched motionless against the snow, his muscles knotted. If they rode his way he would have no chance.

Slowly, ever so slowly, the warriors finished their meal. Then they sat for a moment, two of them with blankets across their shoulders against the chill, and still Justice waited.

Finally they did move, and Justice felt his pulse quicken. His hand tightened on the stag handle of his bowie as he watched the Shoshoni step to their ponies, mounting smoothly, gracefully.

Then the lead rider—a man with an ocher-daubed face—swung toward Ruff, and he crouched lower, hoping that the pony would not pick up his scent. The man kneed his horse forward, and Ruff silently cursed. Then one of the other braves whistled and the rider slowed his mount, turning back to follow the others, who had decided to ford the creek here.

He watched them splash across the stream, their horses' hooves kicking up silver spurs. Then they were into the gray trees beyond, moving like blan-keted ghosts through the shadows.

Still Ruff held his position, not moving for nearly half an hour while the cold wind built to a new rage, drifting the light snow before it. Then, finally, he rose stiffly to his feet, his muscles knotted.

Stumbling forward, Ruff went to the Indian campfire. The ashes were still warm, and he plunged his hands into them—nothing, he decided, could feel so good as warmth. And then he found something else.

One of the Shoshoni had gnawed the meat from his elk bone and thrown it into the fire. Now Ruff had found it, and he lifted it sacramentally. Food—that burned, ash-covered bone was more beautiful than any golden chalice, more precious, and he gnawed greedily at it like some prowling wolf.

There were several ounces of meat left on it—the Shoshoni must be riding high these days. Ravenously he tore the meat from the bone, scooping up handfuls of snow to wash the charcoal-tasting meat down. He stripped the elk rib clean, and still his hunger was hardly satisfied.

He thought of trying to prod the fire to life, but it was risky, and he had no new dry tinder anyway. He had to content himself with sitting near, thrusting his hands once again into the ashes as the snow drifted over him.

But again Justice realized he could not sit still. As much as he would have liked to find a place to hole up, it could be deadly. Not only for him, but for a harmless, black-eyed ghost of a girl who for reasons beyond her comprehension was being dragged into the bloody vortex of danger.

Those Shoshoni Justice had seen—they were riding south, toward Camas.

He walked on, keeping the creek to his right as the day grew darker and the clouds rolled in from the north once more. The wind was at his back, gusting so that twice he stumbled before its force.

It was dusk before he reached Beaverhead, and, exhausted, hungry, freezing, he searched along the banks for any sort of shelter against the bitter night.

Casting back and forth along the bank, he finally found a huge old oak, toppled by another year's storm, its tangled roots thrust toward him like beckoning arms. At the base of the tree was a hollow made when the roots had torn free of the earth, and Justice settled there, the tree partially blocking the wind.

He had no way to make a fire, and no inclination to try it if he had the tools—there was no telling where the Shoshoni had settled in for the night.

The night passed slowly, and Justice waited it out, uncertain if he would survive the cold, the wounds he carried. Saying he did, what kind of shape would he be in to battle McCurdy, the Dentons, the Shoshoni? He had only his knife and little of his strength.

Yet he would go on. He vowed it as he sat sullenly watching the snow drift past, watching the trees shake in the wind.

They had killed him—or thought they had. Justice was damned if he would stay dead for them.

13

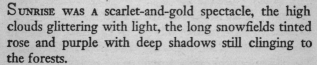

Sᴜɴʀɪꜱᴇ ᴡᴀꜱ ᴀ scarlet-and-gold spectacle, the high
clouds glittering with light, the long snowfields tinted
rose and purple with deep shadows still clinging to
the forests.

Along the horizon to the north all was black and
ominous, and it even bothered Hugh Denton a little.
But only a little—they rested now on a snowy saddleback above the flats, and beyond the ring of spruce
and cedar lay Camas Meadows.

His heart raced greedily as he stepped down from
the wagon bench for a minute, stretching his legs.
McCurdy was staring at him, his pouched eyes flinty,
cold. Hugh smiled, trying to hide his own thoughts,
which were every bit as murderous as McCurdy's.

The only question in Hugh's mind was when. It
had to be done before the gold was recovered, yet not
too soon—McCurdy's guns could be telling if the
Shoshoni came in again.

As he thought of that he let his eyes sweep the
horizon, the timber below. Perhaps the Indians had
gone on to their winter camp. No matter, it would
have to be risked. Hugh had come this far, taken
many chances going all the way back to Baltimore,
and he was not going to give up now.

He knew what McCurdy thought of him and Amos—"greeners," they called them, pilgrims, city boys. But he and Amos were hardly newcomers to the business of fighting, and that was done pretty much the same wherever you went.

They had worked their games along the Baltimore waterfront for years before falling into this scheme; and those wharf rats and seamen were hardly a soft bunch.

There had been more than one knifing and a handful of shootings, plus more knuckle-and-skull bouts than a man could count.

Hugh had let McCurdy think what he wanted—perhaps it would make it easier when the time came. He nodded amiably to McCurdy, who sat his sorrel stiffly, and said, "It's not far now."

McCurdy did not return Hugh's fading smile. If anything, the big man had become more sour with each passing day. The wound in his back had begun to fester, and that did little for his humor.

"Then let's get down there," McCurdy said. "I don't like this. None of it: the weather, the Shoshoni ... you."

Hugh swallowed a curse and clambered back into the wagon box, taking the reins from Marguerite.

"He'll pay for that," he said in an undertone.

Marguerite did not answer. She sat, hands clasped, staring into the snowy distances.

"We'll never make it," she said quietly.

"Don't you believe that," Hugh said with confidence. "We'll make it, and there'll be some high living to repay us for this."

"And Candida?" she asked, turning to him.

"Her!" Hugh laughed and snapped the reins. The wagon creaked down off the saddleback with Amos leading the way. "Don't tell me you're actually starting to worry about her now?"

"No," Marguerite said. Then her eyes flitted back to the dark horizon.

She *was* worried about Candida suddenly—why, she could not have said, except that perhaps she realized belatedly that she and Candida were in the same boat. If Hugh would desert the one, he would likely abandon the other if it came to it.

She glanced at Hugh, trying to convince herself that it was not so, but there was nothing in the hard lines of his face that she found reassuring. She held to the wagon's dashboard as they jolted over a hidden clump of rocks, and she attempted to put it all out of her mind. All but the gold, the high living. . . . It was no good. She couldn't picture San Francisco at all.

She saw McCurdy's bulky form from the corner of her eye, and she looked quickly down. Despite Hugh's conviction, there seemed an equally good chance that McCurdy might win out. She recalled with stark clarity Justice's bleak scenario of what she could expect if McCurdy triumphed, and she shuddered.

Hugh saw her shoulders tremble, and, misunderstanding, he told her, "Don't worry, Marge. Just a little time more and you'll never have to be cold again."

They moved now across the flats, a stand of an acre or so of spruce off to the north. The wind was brisker now; light, powdery snow drifted across the older, packed stuff. Ahead a low line of new mountains showed gray against the darker backdrop of storm clouds.

Suddenly they came upon it, and Hugh halted the team, a reverent curse twisting his lips.

It was a ghostly, chilling landscape, with death the master everywhere. One eye of a skull peered over the snow, and beside it the ribs of a horse jutted up, the drift snow twisting through them. Across the field lay a rusted wagon rim, a half-buried horse's skull, a pair of hoofless pony legs, all scattered by the wolves and scrubbed to ivory by summer sun and autumn rain.

"Damn!" Tim Simmons said. He had stepped down from his bay, and he waited with the others, just looking at the evidence of death and fighting, at the remains of Major Denton's force.

No one moved for a time; they stood there as if at a graveyard's fence, not wanting to enter and disturb the ghosts sleeping now beneath the cold snow.

The wind whistled eerily through the nearby spruce, and Amos, who had never thought of himself as superstitious, felt his skin crawl.

Slowly they walked forward, Amos leading his horse, and for a time they wandered about as if for no purpose. The broken, burned, and splintered tongue of a wagon jutted into the air, already wormy and rotten. Marguerite, who had been walking in circles like the rest of them, suddenly drew up short, and her eyes opened like saucers.

She screamed, and Hugh spun around, his hand going to his gun butt.

"What?" he shouted, running to her. She stood, arm uplifted, a hand to her lips. Hugh looked into the iron-gray tree and saw it—a human skull winking back at them. Wrens had nested in it, and dry grass jutted out of one eyesocket.

"Probably a cougar took it up there," Amos guessed.

Marguerite's scream seemed to have lit a fire under the men, perhaps reminding them that there were

Shoshoni around. Now McCurdy and Tim Simmons dug around the smashed and burned army wagon, using planks torn from the unlucky vehicle.

Hugh, throwing his coat aside, joined them. If the gold was here, it would be in the wagon, he believed, or near it, perhaps tossed aside as the wagon rolled, which it obviously had done.

So if the gold . . . no! No ifs. That gold was there—it had to be. They dug wildly for a time, then fatigue slowed them and their minds fell into patterns once again.

"We'll have to post a lookout," Hugh said as he stood panting next to McCurdy, who had dug the entire tailgate of the army wagon free without finding anything.

"All right—send your brother out," McCurdy said.

"Amos?" Hugh asked, and Amos nodded. Standing guard beat digging in the snow as far as he was concerned.

Hugh put a hand on Amos's shoulder briefly, slowing him, and when McCurdy had gotten back to work, Hugh told him, "Make sure you're on watch when we find that gold, Amos." He kept his voice low. "And when you see it—make sure they can't."

Hugh's eyes were hard, savage, and Amos nodded—he had been with Hugh a long time, and he knew that the man was through playing games, through backing down to McCurdy.

He slogged through the snow, stepping into leather. Then he turned his weary sorrel and rode off into the timber. Hugh glanced at the skies, noting that they had a good three hours of light left, and then he got to it. Alongside McCurdy and Simmons, with none of them speaking, and only the puffing audible, the grunts as they worked, Hugh put his back to it.

Marguerite, with a blue knitted shawl across her

shoulders, her back to the cold gusting wind, watched silently. Suddenly this all seemed so useless, doomed, to her. She thought fleetingly of Justice, remembering when he had offered to return with her to Gallatin. They would have had to winter up there. Gallatin . . . it was a flea-bitten collection of hovels, but it would have been warm there. She would have had all those nights with that tall, mysterious man . . . dead. He was dead!

The idea had never really come home to her. Now, amid the skeletons of man and animal here, death seemed to surround them.

From time to time one of the men would throw a bone aside—an arm which had rested around a woman's shoulder, chopped wood, hugged a kid. . . . She watched Hugh and McCurdy, fascinated by their indifference.

Justice would have written a poem of death.

McCurdy's fingers were bleeding from scraping against the snow, but it hardly slowed him. Suddenly he saw bright metal, and he shoved Hugh aside, clawing at the glittering metal.

He stood, and it gleamed dully in his hand . . . a watch.

Someone's gold watch with the crystal smashed, perhaps telling the time of the attack. Angrily McCurdy slung it aside, and Hugh stood, brushing the snow from his coat, his fists clenching and unclenching. He had stomached all of McCurdy he was going to stomach.

His hand lowered toward his holstered Colt, but he caught himself. Taking a deep breath, he got back to work, saying nothing—he still needed McCurdy for a little while more. Only a little while more.

"This could take forever," Simmons groaned. He leaned back against the wall of the pit he had dug.

"And look at that." He nodded toward the darkening skies. "Damned if it ain't gonna snow again."

"Complaining won't help," Hugh said hotly.

"We could start a fire, melt some of this away," Simmons suggested.

"And nothing would bring the Shoshoni down our throats faster," Hugh snapped.

"I don't think it matters," Simmons said quietly. "I reckon they know we're here anyway, and I reckon they're out there."

"Shut up!" McCurdy snarled. "They ain't out there."

"Sayin' they ain't don't make it so," Simmons answered wearily. Nevertheless he picked up his plank and once again began scraping away the snow.

It was Simmons who found it. Suddenly, unexpectedly, as he worked mired in his own morbid thoughts. Swinging the plank down, he thrust it into the snow and heard the solid thunk.

He froze his motion and glanced around at McCurdy, who had not noticed. Tentatively Simmons dug a little farther, not wanting to sound a false alarm. His mind filled with flashes of anticipation, forebodings, and excitement.

But he was surely wrong—as wrong as McCurdy had been when he had made such a show over the watch. Simmons glanced at Hugh Denton and then at McCurdy again. His plank again thudded against the metal, and Simmons could stand it no longer.

He got to his knees and like a madman began clawing at the snow, throwing it everywhere as he dug. His finger touched a corner of a strongbox, and he turned to say something to McCurdy; but there was no need. The big man hovered over him, his shadow staining the snowbank.

"What is it?" McCurdy asked hoarsely. His eyes

were riveted to the spot where Simmons's hand entered the snow.

"I think it's a strong box," Simmons answered, almost afraid to put the thought into words. "I think it's the gold!"

"Are you sure?" Hugh asked. He scrambled up the bank, his eyes wild.

"No."

Slowly Simmons cleared the snow away, and they watched, afraid of finding it, of not finding that Sacramento gold. Simmons worked as if he were digging eggs from the snow; McCurdy licked his dry lips. Hugh's eyes, which greedily studied the hole Simmons was burrowing in the snow, also flickered meaningfully to the shadows of the spruce forest, where Amos let his sorrel walk slowly forward, noiseless as it crossed the littered snowfield.

McCurdy noticed none of this. He was down on hands and knees now, pawing at the snow with Simmons. A corner of the strongbox appeared. Olive-green, now rust-spotted, the box was of iron, riveted and locked double.

McCurdy and Simmons dragged it to the level ground as Hugh stepped back. Amos sat his horse, watching, his hand slowly finding the hammer of his rifle.

"It's prob'ly not it, prob'ly the wrong box," Simmons said over and over, as if afraid to believe, but his eyes were positively glittering as McCurdy drew his Colt and placed the muzzle to the hasp of the first lock.

"Turn aside," the big man said, and as they did he fired. The lock swung free.

There was a second lock, and for that rusted, heavy lock it took three shots, McCurdy cursing vigorously after each failure. Finally the lock was blown free, whining off through the air to slam into the side of the Denton wagon, and McCurdy's trembling, meaty hand went to the lid, flipping it open.

"God!" McCurdy said with delight.

It was gold, and it shimmered and shone—brilliant yellow in the late sunlight. Mostly coins, there were a few small bars and the remains of canvas sacks rotted away cushioning the eagles and double eagles which lay in neat, rich rows.

McCurdy lifted a double handful of coins into the air and turned toward Hugh, his black eyes as bright as the gold.

Hugh grinned, and Amos made his move, and the day roared with the thunder of guns.

14

McCURDY WAS GRINNING one moment and the next his face was twisted with savagery. He must have already been planning his own move, because his hand was to his Colt before Hugh or Amos could realize what was happening.

McCurdy was quick, but not quick enough to beat a cocked, leveled rifle, and as McCurdy's hand flashed down, Amos triggered off and his bullet slammed into McCurdy's chest, driving the big man back, his face going waxen as Amos fired again, this time missing, his bullet plowing up snow beside McCurdy's head.

McCurdy, enraged, fought back with the strength of madness. He drew his Colt despite a badly damaged arm and from his knees fanned off four shots. One of them tagged Amos, tagged him hard.

Amos tried to fire again, found he could not lift his arm, and screamed out with pain. McCurdy's bullet had torn through his chest, shattering Amos's spine. Now as McCurdy sagged back to the earth, the snow around him stained with crimson, bright with fallen gold coins, Amos toppled over the withers of his sorrel, and the horse, panicked by the shooting, danced off, dragging Amos for a hundred yards before his boot popped free and he came to rest on the snow.

Tim Simmons had been a fraction of a second slower to make his move.

With his eyes wide, he had seen Amos's rifle muzzle explode into a ball of flame, seen McCurdy hit, but Simmons had trouble finding his own revolver beneath his coat.

Now he spun, gun in hand, winging a wild shot at Hugh Denton, who stood there coolly on the bank above him. The bullet whistled past Hugh's ear, and Simmons saw Hugh slowly draw back the hammer of his pistol.

He saw the muzzle train on him, saw the big-bored eye of the barrel, and then he saw no more. Hugh fired, stepped forward, fired again and then again, and Simmons toppled forward, his skull ripped open by one of Hugh's shots, his blood leaking out, steaming against the cold air.

McCurdy was still alive when Hugh turned back.

Alive, but the big man had had it, and he knew it. He sat in the pit, his face as white as the snow. His Colt, only inches away from his hand, seemed impossibly distant.

"Well," he said in a ragged voice, "it was worth a try."

Then Hugh nodded and shot again, and McCurdy felt a flash of searing pain tear his guts open. Then he felt no more.

Hugh tucked his Colt away and jumped into the pit. Marguerite, bewildered, motionless, watched as he scooped up the loose coins. Some of them had McCurdy's blood on them.

"Get down here and help me, dammit!" he shouted at Marguerite.

"I can't!" She looked in horror at McCurdy's body.

"I said get down here! Him—he's just like the rest

of them here. By summer he'll be picked as clean, scattered as far. It's all the same."

"Not to me," Marguerite murmured. But she slid into the pit anyway, keeping her eyes from McCurdy, who sat, wide-eyed, watching them in death.

Together they dragged the heavy strongbox up and over the rim. Hugh was panting heavily by the time they made it. Marguerite had stopped again, staring at Amos, who lay off some distance, unmoving.

"Maybe he's alive."

"You must be crazy," Hugh said in exasperation. "McCurdy cut him in two."

Together they dragged the strongbox to the rear of the wagon, and Hugh let down the tailgate. There was a cold wind gusting, and it caught the flap, whipping it around. Hugh lost his hat.

Glancing toward the skies, he cursed. It was setting up to snow.

The strongbox was a load to get up onto the tailgate. Marguerite helped all she could, but still it nearly slid back and crushed Hugh. He minded none of it—it only meant that there was a wealth of gold in it.

Candida could now look out across the battlefield, and she could see the bloody form of Amos, the scattered bones jutting up from the snow. She began to rock faster, excited by the sight of it.

The runners of that rocking chair slapped furiously against the bed of the wagon as she rocked, her dark eyes wild, her unkempt dark hair flying.

"She can come out now too," Hugh growled. "We've no use for her."

"She's not bothering anything, Hugh," Marguerite protested.

"What's the matter—an attack of conscience, Marguerite?"

"She's not bothering anything," Marguerite repeated.

"She might come out of this one day—then what?"

"She'll never come out of it."

Hugh glanced at Candida. He was inclined to agree with Marguerite about that. "But we can't keep her with us forever," he argued.

"We don't have to." Marguerite gripped his arm. The snow had begun to drift down behind her. "The first small town we come to—we can drop her off. Someone will feed her."

"All right," Hugh said. He agreed only to end the argument. He felt no compassion toward Candida himself. As long as she was disposed of eventually, he couldn't have cared less.

The skies had gone dark. Lightning sputtered across the clouds, lighting their black faces momentarily before the thunder boomed and the snow began in earnest.

"For now, let's get the hell out of here," Hugh said. *South.* He thought only of getting south, and then west, out of these mountains, this wilderness.

The winter would bury their crimes.

As the snow intensified, Hugh whipped his team and drove southward, out of Camas Meadows. McCurdy's horse was tied on behind—the big roan Simmons had been riding had taken off during the shooting, and Amos's sorrel had taken a bullet, crippling it.

For the first two miles he drove the horses to their limit, glancing over his shoulder constantly as if somehow McCurdy could return to pursue them. Then, as the landscape changed and he felt comfortably away from Camas, Hugh slowed the horses, worrying now about keeping them in shape until they hit Dubois . . . wasn't that the first town on their route? He frowned in concentration. Yes, Dubois—then Hugh felt his stomach roll over and his heart stop.

They were there across the road, snow-washed, windswept and savage, their painted face like death's heads.

Shoshoni. They moved slowly toward the Denton wagon, like specters through the twisting snow, silently, eerily forward, their guns in their hands.

There were six of them, and their leader carried a new '73 Winchester, a scalp dangling from the barrel. They appeared and then disappeared behind the screen of snow. Hugh's mind was racing wildly, searching for and finding no solution.

But there seemed no point in surrender, no point in letting the Shoshoni decide his fate. Now, while the storm was thickest, Hugh drove his wagon forward, whipping the horses, driving them right through the line of Indians.

A Shoshoni screamed as the wagon jolted over him. A panicked war pony whinnied and reared up. Hugh fired to either side as he drove through and by them, taking one Shoshoni from his horse.

Then they were through them, and a war whoop filled the air as Hugh frantically whipped the horses onward, through the blinding snow. Twice he fired over his shoulder, directly through the canvas of the wagon, heedless of Candida's safety.

Marguerite clung to the wagon, her face ashen, as they bounced over a rock, splashed across a narrow creek and into the trees beyond. There, abruptly through a brief clearing of the snow, Hugh saw a narrow corridor leading off through the forest and into a rock-walled canyon. Without hesitating he swung the wagon that way, praying that not even a Shoshoni could track him in this wash of snow. Not rapidly, at least.

His offhand shots seemed to have seeded some caution, for leaning far out, he could not see them or hear a horse. They charged on through the timber, breaking into a gravel-strewn canyon where only a few scattered ponderosas grew along the creekbed.

The wheelhorse stumbled, exhausted, and Hugh yanked the reins hard, keeping its head up by main force. The wind roared down the canyon, and the snow fell heavily again. Hugh had to slow the horses, not able to see ten feet ahead of him now.

There was a stand of screening brush, willow and blackthorn, which caught Hugh's eye, and he guided the horses behind it. No sooner had the horses stopped, the wagon still swaying on the springs, than Hugh leaped from the box and frantically cut the harness from the team.

"Hugh!" Marguerite screamed, then leaped far forward and screamed his name again. "Hugh! What are you doing?"

But he didn't answer, he hardly turned his head, but kept working furiously, his eyes flickering to the backtrail.

Then, hurriedly, he led one of the horses to the tailgate. Marguerite followed him, waving her arms futilely in protest. "Hugh . . . ? You can't do this."

He knocked her to the snow and continued. With the cut-away harness Hugh knotted a sort of saddle-pack, and he was dragging the strongbox from the wagon, easing the horse near the tailgate. Then, with desperate strength, he managed to position the strong-box on the horse's back and strap it down as Marguerite watched from the snow, one hand lifted to Hugh, her eyes wide.

The pack was not a good one, but it didn't have to last long. Just enough to make a mile or so. Hugh stepped into the saddle of McCurdy's horse and snatched up the lead to the packhorse.

Marguerite still sat against the ground; the snow twisted past, frosting her dark hair, her shoulders.

"You can't, Hugh! What about me?" she pleaded.

"There's a horse left. Good luck, Marge. See you in Frisco."

Then, with a quick glance down the backtrail, Hugh kneed the horse forward, trailing it out of that blind canyon, the storm swallowing him up.

In bewilderment Marguerite watched him go, and when she could see him no longer she rose, slowly. She started first for the remaining horse, which stood, head bowed, harness in tangles. Then she paused. Turning back to the rear of the wagon, she looked inside.

Candida's eyes did not even shift toward her. She rocked on, Justice's little white dog lying beside her, his head on his paws.

"I . . ." Marguerite started to speak, but there was no point in it. There was nothing more to be done for Candida.

She eased from the tailgate, and suddenly through the snow she saw them coming, four Shoshoni, lances and rifles raised into the air. They whooped as they spotted Marguerite, and they drove down on her from out of the snow.

She turned, slipped to her knees painfully, and ran, her heart in her throat. The horse stood a few yards away now as it wandered, looking for graze, and Marguerite ran for it, all of Ruff's warnings filling her head at once along with the remembrance of that haggard red-haired girl.

She glanced over her shoulder, seeing a brave so near that she could see the white scar on his upper lip, the lusting gleam in his eyes, and she reached desperately for the horse.

She lunged; the horse sidestepped nervously away, and the brave's hand fell on her shoulder, yanking her back as her dress was torn away.

Two of the Shoshoni had leaped from their horses and gone to the wagon—a likely spot for blankets, guns, whiskey. They threw back the canvas and started to jump up.

There she sat.

Candida rocked in her chair, her eyes dark, lifeless, and it seemed that a faint smile played on those full, pale lips.

The Shoshoni who had had his hand on the tailgate, ready to vault into the wagon, froze; his brother, rushing up behind him, emitting shrill war howls, stopped dead in his tracks.

Candida rocked, and they stood motionless before her.

A small white dog, motionless except for his eyes, lay beside her, on his collar two silver tokens which appeared to be coup sticks.

"What is it?" Wonder Hawk shouted. He sat his medicine pony, his buffalo-horn headdress massive, marking him for a medicine chief.

"A woman . . ." Icefall turned toward his medicine man and held the flap aside.

Wonder Hawk leaned low across the withers of his weirdly painted horse and peered into the wagon. Candida rocked madly, her eyes fixed not on Wonder Hawk, not on the distances, but on the middle space which only seers and trance-walkers could perceive.

Icefall looked to his medicine chief, and Wonder Hawk made a sign. "*Na!* It is bad. She is a ghost girl," Wonder Hawk said.

Icefall accepted the medicine chief's word. It was

easy to do so. This woman, so white, so distant, those eyes looking into the third world where the spirits only dwelled . . . Slowly he let the wagon flap down. Then he turned, and with a whoop ran to join the others, to wait for his turn with the white woman in the snow.

Marguerite's screams filled the air at first; then her voice faded to a whimper as one young buck after the other stripped and climbed on top of her, their eyes animal, eager.

She opened her eyes to see a man with a stripe-painted face, a buffalo headdress, and one glinting eye strip and come toward her out of the swirling storm. She screamed again, for the last time, again closing her eyes as he crawled onto her.

Candida rocked on, and the snow cascaded down out of the mottled, lightning-laden skies. The wind was a constant howl in the long canyons.

If Hugh heard Marguerite's screaming, it slowed him not at all; nor did it trouble him. He rode desperately on, yet with growing hope—he seemed to be gaining ground on the pursuing Shoshoni. They would not pursue him much farther south.

Or so Hugh hoped and believed. There was a settlement not thirty-five miles to the southwest. And there was no need to carry the gold that far. The pack horse was laboring heavily under the load, and the jerry-made pack had already broken once and looked to be breaking again.

Hugh stopped on a hillrise and peered through a gap in the clouds toward the canyon below. Nothing. There were no Shoshoni behind him. It would be a simple matter to hide the strongbox. Sure! Hide the box, removing a few pounds of gold for a winter's high living, and return in the spring with two mules.

The wind shrieked. Hugh whistled as he pulled the

strongbox from the horse's back, letting it drop to the earth. A few coins spilled out, and Hugh knelt to pick them up, his eyes going constantly to the surrounding trees.

He shoved the coins into his pocket and then dragged the strongbox off the trail and up into a huge jumble of snow-draped boulders. There, poking around, he found a crevice.

Hugh dropped a rock into the crevice, which was three feet wide, tapering down. The rock clicked reassuringly off the sides and then clattered against the bottom. No more than five feet down then—good! He dragged the strongbox to the crevice and heaved it in, watching with satisfaction as it wedged itself between the stone walls. Then he hurriedly covered the opening with brush and pine litter. In hours the snow would cover even that, obliterating all signs of Hugh's tampering.

With satisfaction he stood, patting the gold coins which rested heavily in his coat pockets. Then he slid from the boulder, landing hard. He stood, taking a deep breath, and hobbled toward his horse.

There was another horse!

Hugh frowned and looked twice. He knew that horse well—the big roan Tim Simmons had been riding. Simmons!

No, that was absurd. Simmons was dead. Still, Hugh was unsettled. The horse had run off during the fight at Camas. Now it had undoubtedly simply followed them and reappeared at this unlikely moment.

That was all there was to it.

"Of course," Hugh breathed. He wiped his forehead and walked to the sorrel. "What a case of nerves I'm getting."

He laughed again, under his breath, and reached for the reins to his horse.

It was then that the tall man stepped out from behind the trees and stood facing Hugh Denton. It was Justice, and he had a gun. Hugh backed away a step, his eyes wide, his heart pounding.

"Did you get enough gold to last you, Hugh?" Ruff asked as he took another step forward. "Enough gold to last you in hell?"

15

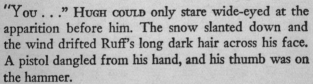

"You . . ." Hugh could only stare wide-eyed at the apparition before him. The snow slanted down and the wind drifted Ruff's long dark hair across his face. A pistol dangled from his hand, and his thumb was on the hammer.

Hugh felt his hand trembling—it had always been Justice that he feared, sensing a steel in the man that a dog like McCurdy did not have. And now he stood there, ready to kill, to repay the botched assassination in kind.

But Justice would not botch the job; Hugh knew it, and his mind went cold. Desperately he made an offer. "There's plenty of gold there for both of us."

Ruff didn't even answer, as Hugh knew he would not. The plainsman stood there, eyes alert, motionless in the wind.

"Whenever you feel lucky, Hugh," Ruff said calmly.

"Why . . . you don't have to shoot me! I'll surrender. Sure—you can take me back to Fort Lincoln. I'll stand trial."

"What's the use, Hugh? You'd hang for any one of half a dozen things you've done. Besides, I'm no lawman. I'm just a man you tried to kill. You should have done it, Hugh. You should have done it right."

Hugh smiled nervously. "You wouldn't just cut me down." He laughed. "I know you, I know your kind—you couldn't."

But he looked into those cold blue eyes and he was not certain at all. Ruff came another step forward. Behind him the trees swayed in the wind.

"I'll just toss my gun away," Hugh said with a shrug. "I'm gambling that I know you, Justice. . . ."

But Ruff could read it in his eyes. Throw that gun away? Not likely.

Hugh wanted that gold, he wanted it more than he wanted to live, and his hand, which had been gingerly inching toward the walnut butt of his holstered Colt, now swept down as Hugh made his play. He had the Colt in his hand, had the hammer back, and he smirked triumphantly.

He had beaten Justice.

Why then was the man still standing there? Smoke seemed to be curling up from the muzzle of Justice's gun—that was impossible. Hugh had heard no gunshot—only those two claps of thunder.

But now he felt his legs turn to rubber, and he felt a pain in his chest as if someone had shoved a red-hot poker through his lungs.

He was damned if he'd go out alone.

Hugh tried to raise the gun, tried to pull the trigger, but it was like an anvil in his hand, and Justice was still coming forward, wavering crazily. Triumphantly, Hugh brought the Colt level, a last smile on his thin, blistered lips.

And then that distant thunder boomed again, and Hugh saw a flash of brilliant light. He thought he had been struck by lightning. The heat of it, the force . . . and then the cold returned, and he opened his eyes, finding that he was on his back against the cold earth.

The trees wavered in the wind; the snow fell. And Justice stood over him, only watching as the dark clouds rolled across the earth.

"Where's Candida?" Justice demanded.

Hugh blinked. Sweat rolled across his cheeks—or was it melted snow? They were tears, and angrily he blinked them away. He did not answer, but his eyes rolled back toward the canyon where the wagon rested.

Then he looked back toward Justice—surprised to see three of him. A hundred, a thousand—all with painted faces and smoking guns. And then even that crazy bit of reality was washed away by the storm.

Ruff stepped into the saddle of Simmons's sorrel and took the reins to Hugh's horse. Then he rode slowly out toward the canyon, the horses picking their way around Hugh's body.

The snow still fell, and day was dark as dusk. There were drifts five feet or more deep in the cuts, and Ruff had to pick his way slowly downward, his eyes alert for Shoshoni, the storm-camouflaged wagon.

If the Shoshoni had found the wagon . . . and then he saw it. The snow was deep around it. A heavy wind was drifting it up on the north side.

Cautiously Justice walked his horses forward. He saw no sign of the Indians, but that meant nothing. He splashed across an icy, quick-running rill and climbed the far bank.

Justice came up the long valley with the wind in his face, the horses moving silently across the snow. The wagon looked undisturbed, deserted. If they had taken Candida . . .

He swung down and went to the tailgate, swinging the flap back.

Dooley Dog was instantly to his feet, bounding into Ruff's arms, and Ruff held him, scratching his faithful head. Candida still sat there in that thin chemise, rocking away in her world where time, distance, danger had no meaning.

"Thank God you're all right—"

And then the gun thundered. A bullet whipped through the canvas, tearing the sidewall to jagged splinters. A second shot dug a raw groove in the floorboard.

Justice leaped from the wagon, wanting to keep the bullets away from Candida. It was Ruff the gunman wanted, and now he knew why, knew who this sniper was.

Ruff had hit the ground on the run and dashed behind the willow brush, going to his belly against the cold snow, his Colt in his hand.

The rifle fired again, whining off the wagon's front wheel, and Ruff frowned. He recognized that rifle's sound—the man behind the sights was the man who had killed Fire Sky and Cada, the night rider who had met with the Dentons away back down the trail.

Ruff took a breath, bunched his muscles, and lunged for the trees some fifty feet away. He zigzagged as he ran, and a shot narrowly missed him as he leaped for the timber, panting, his eyes searching the snowy hillside for the telltale rising smoke of the sniper's rifle.

He saw nothing through the wash of the storm, but he studied the hillside carefully, searching for a likely position. The rifleman would want cover and he would want elevation. There were several possibilities, but only the granite outcropping some two hundred yards up seemed near enough.

There a man would have height enough, but be near enough for sure-thing shooting. The outcropping was perhaps fifty feet across, ringed around by aspen and spruce.

Was that his position? The only way to be sure was to move, and that could be deadly. Justice studied it for a time longer, trying to find a good approach—he was not underestimating this man, for he had seen his work.

The clouds, scudding in low over the valley, were intermittent. And now as a cloud settled in, Ruff made his dash, moving through the cold fog across the river bottom, making the far side before the cloud gapped and a moment's brilliant light brightened the valley.

Panting, his chest throbbing dully where he had torn it open again, Justice pressed against the rocks, ankle-deep in snow, looking upward. He had not been seen, or thought he had not.

The sniper had not fired, but perhaps he was only cautious, expertly careful. Justice did not forget for a moment that this man had taken down two battle-experienced Crow warriors, and he had picked off Fire Sky at what must have been five hundred yards from elevation.

Ruff wished for his own Spencer, lost in the fall from the bluff—but wishing would win no prize, and so, with Colt in hand, he planted a boot and scaled the rocks, moving through the snow-heavy brush, the ice-laden trees, as the clouds rolled over.

He saw something and froze. Above and to the left, among the cedar, and he stared into the shadows, eyes blinking. Someone . . . or was it only cloud shadow?

He was motionless for a long moment, then, not wanting to let the man get away this time, he forced himself to move. It was a short distance to the heavy cover of the cedar forest, the trunks of the trees seeming inordinately red against the dark background, the clouds.

It was a forest without life. Normally gray squirrels would have been chattering in the trees, deer moving softly through the shadows—but not in this weather. Nothing moved, except for the hunter.

There was twenty yards of open space between Ruff and the cedars. Once he achieved the forest, he was confident he could circle to the outcropping, and he believed he was cutting off all escape—there was no way a horse could make that rocky, sheer western face.

The trick was making the cedars.

He steeled himself and made his move. He took three running strides and then the rifle boomed again, tearing a chunk of leather from his bootheel, and Justice went into a headlong dive, crawling into the underbrush as the bullets searched among the cedars for him.

Justice sat against an ice-glazed cedar for a moment. His breath was coming raggedly at this altitude, and for a moment he thought he had been hit—but it was only the insistent pain of the broken ribs, and he swallowed the pain, rising shakily to his feet, moving in a crouch across the shadowed ground beneath the cedars.

Now the game was different—now the rifleman knew where Justice was. But he also knew Ruff was stalking him. It could make the man a little nervous.

It was a waiting game; that man was going nowhere unless he went past Ruff . . . or through him.

But Ruff had the feeling that this sniper was not the kind to try him head-on. He was a hunting man, a man good with a rifle, good at picking and choosing. Now Ruff must not let him pick his spot, choose his moment. He must pressure him, force a mistake, and so Ruff kept moving, weaving through the forest, with only the faint whishing sounds of snow underfoot, of the damp brush against his buckskins.

Then suddenly he was there. The outcropping jutted out into space, gray, empty. Then where was the sniper? Of course he could have slipped past Justice in the snow, but Ruff did not believe it. There had been many an Indian, many a mountain man, who had tried it, and Ruff did not believe this man was that good.

And then he was there. He loomed up from behind a clump of brush, and his rifle went to his shoulder. But that rifle, the sniper's edge at long distance, was too slow for close-in work, and Ruff's Colt came up, speaking with the voice of hell, spewing flame as the bullets slammed into the sniper, one tearing open his face, a second unhinging his shoulder as Ruff moved forward.

The rifle boomed once, a random shot which winged off into the cedars, and then it spoke no more.

Ruff went to him, his gun still smoking, and he stood over Solomon Turk, who was bleeding profusely, his face ripped open from one of Ruff's shots.

"Damn you," the big man managed to say through the choking blood. "Damn you to hell, you fancy bastard."

"It's all your doing, Turk. You dug your own grave."

"You slept with my woman. Madeline told me! Told me like she was proud."

"Then she wasn't your woman, I guess. Was she, Turk?" Justice holstered his gun, picking up Solomon Turk's fancy engraved Spencer. "Besides, I've a notion that you did it for the money Hugh promised you more'n for Madeline. It's a long cold trek out here. Hell, if you'd've wanted to be with her . . . if she'da wanted to be with you, to be your woman . . . well, I guess you would have stayed at Fort Lincoln."

Turk's eyes brightened unnaturally. His face was a bloody mess of shattered bone and torn-up muscle, but Justice thought he read a brief smile on the Turk's face as he replied.

"I guess maybe you're right, Ruff . . . you see, I . . ."

Whatever it was that Turk had to say, he never finished it. Death closed his eyes, and Ruff stood, feeling no pity for the man. He had killed better than he was, and from long range, pitilessly.

The wind had shifted, and it was on Ruff's right shoulder as he came down from off the mountain. Night was closing rapidly, and the tiny valley was smothered by darkness.

There was no point in trying to run anywhere, no point in hiding. Likely the Shoshoni, having everything they thought worth taking, had once again swung northward, riding to their winter lodges.

The snow drifted past as Ruff reached the wagon. Scooping out a hollow in the snow, beneath the wagon, Ruff built a fire, using some of the siding from the wagon itself—come morning they would ride out on horseback, one way or the other.

Just now there was the cold to be considered above all else. That wagon had never been much account anyway.

Ruff climbed into the deeply shadowed wagon and went to Candida, untying her from the chair. She was limp in his arms as he picked her up and, slipping from the wagon, sat her beside the fire.

Dooley was there, and he went to Candida, nuzzling her lifeless hand. Ruff frowned.

"You mean you finally found a person worth caring for, dog?"

The night grew cold and chill. Ruff noticed that Candida was trembling, and he scooted beside her, putting his arm around her as they watched the comforting fire, as the night went obsidian black, silent.

"It's over," Ruff told Candida. Her eyes sparked with the firelight, and he hugged her more tightly. "Candida, I mean it's really all over—or should be. Your father—he's lyin' dead back there, and I'm sorry about it. I reckon he was a good man, but the good die as well.

"He wouldn't have wanted to see you this way, girl."

But Candida did not respond, and Ruff could only hold her tight in the darkness, sharing a blanket as the red fire flickering in the wind kept night away.

Where they sat, under the tailgate of the wagon, the snow did not hit them, and the howling wind was cut. By morning, Ruff guessed, this storm might be blown out. It seemed quieter than it had been, and once he saw for an instant a distant, blue crystal star through a break in the foaming clouds.

He rocked Candida in his arms, staring deeply into the fire, which hid many messages and which fully revealed none as it bent and twisted in the wind, red going to gold, gold to smoke, rising into the dark skies.

Quietly then he recited to her:

"In your eyes I saw great beauty,
    Eyes that once were star-caressed
    And love-lit, laughing, vital, blessed.
On your lips I saw a faded smile—
    Lips which used to laugh, now dressed
    In silent sorrow, loneliness.
Come out of winter, silent bird,

Let your summer song be heard,
And my lips touch your silent lips . . ."

And then the voice, so frail and distant supplied the final line: "So they may live again."

Then slowly Candida's head turned toward Ruff, and he looked deeply into her eyes. Those eyes! They lived, sparked, flashed with fire.

A long journey out of night had ended, and she sat there, only a small, shaken woman with beautiful lips and deep, black eyes.

"Was it really you?" Justice asked.

"Me?" She smiled, a smile that died away as quickly as a golden spark from the fire. "Yes—it was I who spoke. And it was you who accomplished it. You who led me forth. . . ." Her eyes searched this tall, dark man, this stranger who had been her only friend.

Ruff squeezed her shoulder, and he smiled at her, a smile which Candida returned—only this time it was no short-lived expression, but a long, warm smile which produced a lingering glow.

"And now," Ruff said. "Now that you are back. You must be hungry. Curious."

She simply gazed at him, liking those cool blue eyes, the broad shoulders of Ruff Justice.

"What can I get you? What can I do for you, Candida?"

And she smiled and rested her head against his shoulder before she said, quietly:

"Let your lips touch my silent lips, so they may live again."

And he did.

WESTWARD HO!

The following is the opening section from the
next novel in the gun-blazing, action-packed new
Ruff Justice series from Signet:
RUFF JUSTICE #2: NIGHT OF THE APACHE

1

THE LAND WAS a savage, raw thing. Barren stretches
of empty land broken by reddish, wind-sculpted
spires and stark mesas. There were blistered, grassless
plains where nothing but a coyote could scratch a living, and deep arroyos where water ran but once a
year—destructively, tearing great boulders from their
moorings, uprooting the few trees which grew across
the land.

The tall man with the long dark hair stood on a
dusty knoll, looking out across the Arizona desert
with probing, ice-blue eyes. It seemed to him that
nothing lived upon the desert which was not barbed,
hard-shelled, or poisonous. It was likely that the men
who dwelled here were much the same.

It was a far cry from the Colorado Rockies or the
grassy Dakota plains. The sun was a shimmering ball
of white heat against a pale sky. Each breath was arid,

dusty. What water Justice had found had been alkali-laden, bitter or too silty to drink. Yet the people clustered around that water, clinging to it for life. Out there—his eyes lifted to the parched distances—out there there was no life.

"This will take some getting used to, horse," Justice said. He poured a little water from his canteen into his hat, and the big gray gelding he rode drank it eagerly.

Ruff's buckskins clung to him, sweat trickled down his throat and across his forehead, stinging his eyes. He leaned against the gray a time longer, stretching the kinks out, and then he stepped into leather once more. Taking his bearings by the low, massive mesa to the north and west, he continued on, toward Fort Bowie.

As the tall man rode, he studied the lay of the land, eager to know all he could learn as quickly as he could learn it. This would be no hayride. The land was hostile and rife with hostile men. The Mescalero Apache were kicking up their heels again, and they were to be the enemy.

The Mescalero, of whom it was said no finer guerrilla fighter had ever walked the face of the earth. Men who came with the wind and were gone with it, dusty silent fighters who could live off this barren land. It was said they preferred to fight on foot, but were consummate horsemen.

Justice had taken great pains to learn about the Mescalero. He was familiar with their religion, their history, their art. Undoubtedly much of what he had learned would stand revision, for much of it was secondhand, yet he was a step ahead of the game.

One thing he had determined: To attempt to fight the Apache without a knowledge of his ways was akin to suicide. And the land itself—all new, raw, rugged. He had familiarized himself as much as possible with the ways of the land as well. Yet not many men had ridden this land, or successfully lived off it, and the information was hard to come by.

"Next time," Ruff told the gray, whose ears pricked with curiosity, "I'll keep my hands on the table."

For Ruff had no doubt what had precipitated this journey. That damned Captain Cavendish back at Fort Kearney just had to be drinking that night of the officer's ball, and Ruff just had to walk in at the wrong time with his report to Colonel Mitchell.

Cavendish had looked up at the tall, wavy-haired scout dressed in white buckskins and broad-brimmed hat with a red plume and made a remark.

Something about the "fancy boys," as Ruff recalled it. He had let it go by and taken a seat beside the colonel. Then there had been a second remark, and Ruff couldn't hold it back.

It was later that he found out Cavendish was related to the colonel—when Cavendish, with that bandage across his broken nose, stood beside Mitchell while Ruff was offered a choice.

Arizona or out of army service.

He had been angry enough to think of telling Mitchell what he could do with all of Arizona, but second thoughts had caused Ruff to accept the assignment. It was a challenge, and it had been time to move on anyway.

Ruff halted the gray, and, leaning forward across the withers, he mopped his forehead.

"There it is," he said to the gray. "Home for a time. Not much to look at, is it?"

The gray lifted its head as if understanding. Probably it smelled others of its kind, even at that distance. Fort Bowie—what there was of it—stood on level ground below them.

A palisade of logs freighted in from somewhere distant encircled a collection of low-roofed, weathered buildings. There were three stone structures inside the walls—probably the headquarters building, the armory, and the brig.

Just outside the walls was a slovenly jumble of shacks and rough adobes. There were two unpainted, new buildings of sawn lumber—saloons, undoubtedly.

"I've seen worse," Ruff said. Then, straightening his hat, he rode down off the bare knoll toward the fort, the low evening sun sketching long shadows before him.

The sun had sunk behind the long line of saw-toothed mountains to the south before Ruff made the main gate. A rose-colored flush clung to the amber sands; the cottonwoods near the river were deep in shadow. Dove winged homeward across the sundown skies.

They were just closing the stockade gate as Ruff rode up, his stomach paying attention to the smells of beans and bacon cooking somewhere. A blue-jacketed guard appeared on the parapet, and he called down a challenge.

"Who goes there?"

"Ruffin T. Justice, scout, reporting in to Colonel Lasseman."

There was a moment's silence, and then the high gate swung open again, creaking on iron hinges, and Ruff kneed the big gray forward into the fort. A sergeant with a cradled Winchester stood looking up at Ruff, his florid face expressionless, dusty.

"Colonel's at supper," the sergeant informed Justice. "His quarters are behind the armory if you can't wait till morning." The man nodded toward the large stone building. Behind it a faintly yellow frame dwelling sat, smoke rising lazily from a native stone chimney.

"Thanks," Ruff said. Then he clicked his tongue

and the gray tracked across the parade ground, tiny puffs of dust rising from its hoofs.

"Isn't that something?" the sergeant said to the guard who stood beside him. The corporal's eyes lifted to study the tall man in buckskins, noticing the long hair curling down his back, the red plume protruding from the band of that wide hat.

The corporal only shrugged, returning to his watch. The sergeant shook his head slightly, and after glancing once at the dusk-shadowed mountains, he turned and walked toward the barracks, wondering what Casqual would give to liberate *that* hair.

There was a light in the window of the colonel's house when Justice swung down, and the smell of beef cooking in the air. He dusted himself off, loosened the gray's cinches, and stepped onto the front porch, running his fingers through his hair as he did so.

Ruff knocked on the door and waited, back to it, watching the last glow of sunset, listening to the sounds of marching feet which reached his ears from somewhere across the camp.

The door opened, and he turned to meet a startlingly green pair of eyes. Green they were, and alluring, set in a pretty face. A young woman with full, ripe breasts and voluptuous hips stood there, her slightly full mouth pursed expectantly.

"I'm here to report to Colonel Lasseman," Ruff said slowly. His eyes swept up and down the woman as he spoke, and when he met her eyes again, they were amused, bright with enticement.

"Come in," she answered. "The colonel is at supper. . . . I'm Mrs. Lasseman," she added with what Ruff read as a touch of reluctance.

He stepped in, ducking a little to clear the low lintel, and with his hat in his hand, he followed her across the interior of the cozy, neat parlor.

Colonel Lasseman was in the room beyond, at his supper table. He lifted bleary eyes to Justice as his wife led the tall man into the room.

Lasseman had close-cropped steel-gray hair and slack features surrounding a harsh, small mouth. He wore a napkin tucked into his shirt collar just now. His tunic lay on the floor beside him—a bit of carelessness which caused Ruff's eyes to narrow slightly.

Ruff had known many army men, good, bad and indifferent. But nothing was more rare than a slovenly officer—especially a high-ranking man whose life had been based on structure, order, discipline.

"Who are you?" Lasseman grumbled.

"Ruffin T. Justice," the tall man replied. He took another step forward and stood erectly across the table from the colonel, his cool blue eyes meeting Lasseman's gaze for a moment. "I've orders from General Franklin—"

"I know all about it." Lasseman waved a disgusted hand. "I recall now . . . I didn't think you'd be here so soon."

The tone of his voice suggested a hope that Ruff might never show up at all. Lasseman's eyes swept over Justice, trying to measure the man. He sighed, as if to say, "What did I do to deserve *this?*" Then he returned to his steak.

"Sit down, Justice, sit down."

Ruff nodded and took a seat. When he glanced up those green eyes of Mrs. Lasseman were on him. She smiled, faintly.

"Would you like some coffee, Mr. Justice?"

"There's nothing I'd appreciate more just now," he replied with a smile.

Lasseman glanced up sharply; he looked from Justice to his wife and then back down at his plate, where nothing but a bone and gravy remained.

After the woman had left the room, the colonel said in a gravelly voice, "I don't like troublemakers, Mister Justice."

"Nor do I, sir. I'm here because of one."

"Yes . . ." Lasseman shook his head slightly, then turned and without leaving his chair fished a cigar from the bureau behind him. "Smoke?"

Ruff shook his head. He watched as the colonel took his time lighting the cigar, holding it over his match for a long minute before finally shaking out the flame and poking the black cigar between his fleshy lips.

Mrs. Lasseman had returned with a coffee pot and two cups. She poured silently and then was gone again, with only the slightest glance at Justice.

"As I say," Lasseman remarked again, "I don't like troublemakers, Mr. Justice. I've got plenty of trouble trying to hold down this corner of Arizona without the extra aggravation.

"I've got a renegade Apache named Casqual who likes to ride around the territory lifting people's hair, butchering and burning. I've got a thousand like him under land arrest out back." His finger pointed toward some vague, distant location. "I've got weary troopers, an incompetent surgeon, few supplies, and a whole lot of empty territory out there where anything could be happening right now . . . and probably is," he added meditatively.

"What's it all about?" Ruff wanted to know.

"What?" Lasseman glanced up, not understanding.

"What's Casqual's complaint? Why is the Apache warring?"

"It's an Indian's nature, sir. I thought a man with your experience knew that. Hell, these savages have been warring among themselves since the day the Lord planted their red feet on this continent. If they'd had the weaponry of Europe to use on each other, there'd not be a red man alive today. It's their nature, sir, and their inclination."

"I don't buy that," Ruff said.

"You don't buy it? You don't have to buy it, Justice! But it's the way it is—Casqual is a bloodthirsty, murdering savage."

"What you say is partly true," Ruff said, leaning forward, folding his hands on the table. "The Indian way was a way of war—like that of all mankind seems to be. But he knows now that he's up against something he can't whip. He's been willing to make peace for the most part.

"Then there's been a series of broken promises, the extinction of the buffalo, the taking of land—"

"You'll not see anybody fighting Casqual for that damned desert land, Justice. It's a world where no white man will ever live. Let him have it and be damned. Nor have there ever been enough buffalo in Arizona to shake a stick at. There's little graze, less water. No." He shook his head definitely. "Casqual has no motives but viciousness. I know." He winked.

"And the others?" Ruff wanted to know.

"The others." Lasseman sighed and stood, going to the sideboard, where he poured himself a tumbler of whiskey. "You mean the reservation Apaches. Mostly they don't seem to care for reservation life, being cooped up. But dammit, Justice, if they were let off they'd join up with Casqual in a minute!

"Just why in hell are you so interested? Are you a scout or a missionary, Justice?"

"I'm a scout, colonel. But it's a fool who fights an unknown enemy. I want to know the situation here, to know Casqual's tendencies, his strengths and weaknesses . . ."

The colonel snorted. "Never bothered Gusty any."

"Gusty?"

"Gusty Winds. Gustav Windt's his real name—he's my regular scout, and a good one. He can track, live off the desert . . . and he can fight. Can you fight, Justice? Will you?"

Justice's eyes narrowed, and he said, "There's a copy of my service record in that envelope with my orders."

"It's not personal, Justice," the colonel said, though the way he said it made Ruff think it was already partly personal. He watched as Lasseman poured another stiff drink for himself.

"I didn't think it was," Ruff answered.

"But I've got a scout already. Three, counting the Navajo Windt works with. And, like I say, he's done the job for me. I can't imagine why General Franklin sent you on down here." He scanned Ruff's orders, shrugging finally.

"It could be that despite your fine scouts, colonel, you've still got Casqual running around the territory."

"And you'll find him?" Lasseman laughed.

"Oh, I'll find him, and I'll bring him in. It may take me some time, colonel, but you can bet I'll find the man."

Lasseman stood looking at the tall man opposite him, those cold blue eyes, the determined lines of his face, and he was damned if he didn't believe that Justice had what it would take to bring Casqual in.

"Goodnight, sir," Justice said, placing his hat on his head, and Lasseman nodded in return as the big mustached plainsman turned and strode toward the door.

The door closed behind Justice, and after a moment

the colonel's wife came into the room, a faint smile playing on her full lips.

"He's quite a man, isn't he?"

"Too much of a man, Carry," Lasseman said. "Too much of a man for you to tame, too much for me perhaps. But not for the desert." The colonel finished his drink with a grimace. "The desert will take care of Mr. Justice, the desert and Casqual—and the sooner the better, I think."

"Still . . ." Carry Lasseman fell silent. She walked to the window, her husband's eyes on her slender back, and she drew the curtains aside just enough to watch the tall man leading his gray horse across the packed earth of the parade ground before the star-cast shadows swallowed him up.

She felt her husband at her shoulder and turned to look up at him. He smelled of salt perspiration, tobacco, and raw whiskey. He leaned forward, peering out the window himself.

"Have your look, Carry. Have yourself a good long look at Mr. Justice."

"Why, Hugh . . ." She laughed, a laugh which broke off in panic as Lasseman's hand shot out and went to the back of her head, grabbing a handful of her auburn hair. Angrily he jerked her head around, pressing her face savagely against the glass pane.

"Look," he panted in her ear. "Dammit! Look at him, Carry, because I swear you'll not have him to look at for long!"

Slowly she felt his hand loosen its grip, but she did not dare to move for a long minute. She stood with her face still pressed against the smooth, cool glass, her heart pounding like a hammer until she heard him walk away, crossing to the liquor cabinet.